MW01125948

Breaking All the Rules

Rhonda McKnight

Copyright © 2014 by Rhonda McKnight Nain
All rights reserved. No part of this book may be reproduced in any form or by any means without prior consent of the author, excepting brief quotes used in reviews.

This is a work of fiction. Any references or similarities to actual events, real people, living or dead, or to real locales are intended to give the story a sense of reality. Any similarity in other names, characters, places and incidents is entirely coincidental.

ISBN: 1496155718
ISBN-13: 978-1496155719

God Cares Creations
P.O. Box 825
Ellenwood, GA 30294

Also by Rhonda McKnight

Secrets and Lies

An Inconvenient Friend

What Kind of Fool

A Woman's Revenge

Give A Little Love

Table of Contents

Dedication

In loving memory of
Mrs. Jacqueline "Quilla" Hurd Harris
July 31, 1934 - September 5, 2013
I'm so glad you had a chance to read this story and that it gave you joy.

Acknowledgements

My readers - You encouraged me to get back in front of the laptop for something other than Facebook. Thanks for loving my work and encouraging me to give you another story.

Thanks to my author buddies Sherri Lewis, Tia McCollors and Tiffany L. Warren for reminding me that I'm a writer when I'd forgotten.

Thanks to my dear friend, Janice Ingle, for always giving me the feedback I need on my projects and the sister-girlfriend support I need in every other area of my life. I love you!

Thanks always to my sons, Aaron and Micah for being the wind beneath my wings.

Chapter 1

I hadn't heard the words that came out of my sister's mouth correctly. Her statement almost made me drop my brand new seven hundred dollar phone in the toilet. I pulled it away from my ear, set it on the knee wall next to the commode and pushed the speaker button.

"I know you're probably shocked, but I'm so happy I could cry!"

I closed my eyes to the sound of her voice. She hadn't said what I thought she'd said. She hadn't said she was marrying Terrance Wright. She couldn't have said that.

"Deniece, I know you're there. I can hear those stupid wind chimes in your bathroom window."

I peeked over my shoulder at the noisy ornament that had betrayed me and smirked. Even though she knew I was still present, I considered pushing the end button and pretending the call had dropped, but there was no point in doing that. Pesky as she was, she'd only call back until I answered.

I swallowed, lowered the toilet seat lid and plopped my "needed to lose twenty pounds" behind down. "I'm here," I croaked like I'd sucked in a room full of dry air.

"I know you're surprised, because who would have thought I'd be interested in your leftovers, but it's a long story how we really got to know each other and although I feel kind of bad that he's kinda ex-ish for you, I can't help but be happy because I've found the man I want to spend the rest of my life with."

I shook my head. This was crazy. Way out there for a

pre-coffee conversation. Kind of ex-ish? Had my sister lost her mind?

"He proposed last night. I was going to call you when I got home but it was close to midnight and I can never remember if you're in a different time zone."

I rolled my eyes. "New York is on the east coast just like you are, Janette, but I was asleep at midnight so I appreciate you holding off on your news," I refused to say good, "until this morning."

"I have so much to do. I need your help like yesterday. Do you think we could talk about some wedding stuff?"

I stared at the phone, tempted once again to push the end button and disconnect the call. "No, boo. I'm not even dressed and I have an appointment to get to, so I most definitely can't talk about this right now. I'll call you later."

"Wait!" Janette shrieked. "There's one more thing. I need a favor."

My baby sister was and had always been oblivious to my feelings. It would never occur to her to ask, "*Are you okay with me marrying the only guy you have ever loved?"*

I swallowed again. This lump nearly choked me going down, because it was a knot full of regrets. My sister didn't really know that much about my relationship with Terrance. I'd done much too good of a job denying and disguising that fact all those years ago to really hold her accountable for my heartache, but still, the backstabber knew there was a rule most women held fast to…never date your girl's exes. Surely, she knew the rule applied to sisters as well.

"What's the favor?" I asked, rolling off a few sheets of toilet paper. I wanted to cry, but I didn't dare ruin my makeup. I had to be out of the door at a meeting with a new client in fifteen minutes.

"I need you to come home as soon as possible and pull

the wedding together for me."

I popped to my feet like someone had sprung me from a Jack-in-the-box. "Janette Malcolm," I said, using the sir name we shared. "I know you aren't asking me to plan a wedding for you and my ex-boyfriend."

Janette's spoiled attitude came through on the phone. "Why not? You're a wedding planner and it's not like he's a new ex. There's a string of exes between him and you."

I fought to keep my mouth shut, because my temper was rising. My sister continued. "And besides the favor is for me not him. I'm the one who needs the help. All Terrance will do is get a tux and show up."

Terrance in a tux, the image took me back to high school. Specifically, to prom night, which was the last time, I'd seen Terrance in a tuxedo. He'd been wearing it for me, because he was my date. How crazy that the next time I'd see him in one he'd have my sister on his arm. That wasn't right. In fact, it was all kinds of wrong.

I picked up the phone, walked into my closet and removed the dress I was planning to wear. "I'm really booked out right now. There's no way I can fit an out of state wedding in my schedule. Hire a local wedding planner."

"I don't have money for a wedding planner," Janette protested, "and the only one who is the least bit reasonable is booked up for our date."

"Choose another date. I mean, it's not like you guys can't move it. He just asked you to marry him last night."

"We can't move the date." Janette hesitated. There was a nervous pause in the air and then she continued, "The wedding is in a month."

"A month?" I dropped my dress. The hairs stood up on the back of my neck. "Why the rush?"

"We need to have it really soon. Remember, I said I had two things to tell you?" Janette paused again. "I'm six months pregnant."

***

Gayle Lincoln, my best friend and personal assistant hovered over my desk. "Are you going to do it?"

I took a deep breath. "I don't think I have a choice."

Gayle crossed her arms in front of her chest. "Of course you do. We all have choices."

"She's my sister." I dropped my eyes to the paperwork in front of me. I could sense Gayle rolling hers above me.

"She's being unfair." Gayle tapped the end of her pen on the desk as if to get my attention. "If she's going to marry him, which I suppose she nearly has to at this point, she should at least have the decency to do it in Vegas or something."

I had considered suggesting that or even a wedding honeymoon combination on a tropical island or cruise ship, but Janette was too pregnant for that kind of travel. Even if she wasn't, she wouldn't do it. I raised my eyes to meet Gayle's. "You don't know Janette. She's dreamed of having a big wedding her entire life. Every year, when we were children, she'd get a wedding dress for her Barbie doll. She's been watching those wedding and Bridezilla shows for years."

"So, I repeat, she should plan something small if she can't hire someone to handle it."

I tightened my grip on the arms of my chair. "I know I sound crazy, but at the end of the day, after the wedding is done and even after she has the baby, she's still going to be my sister. That's never going to change. I don't have much family. I can't cut her off over a man, even if he was mine." I rolled my eyes.

Gayle grunted like she always did when she was frustrated with me. "I'm not saying cut her off. I'm saying tell her off. Be angry. Let her know how you feel."

"What's getting all worked up on the phone going to solve?"

"You'll be able to check it off the to-do list before you get to Garrison. You don't want to blow up there. You'll be in the same house."

I picked up my cell phone and pushed the gallery icon for the picture Janette had sent to me just this morning. It was a sideways view of her belly. The corners of my mouth turned up. I shook my head. "Fighting isn't good for pregnant women."

"Puleeze, pregnant women don't get a pass on everything."

I sighed and threw up my hands. "You've met her. She's fragile."

Gayle pinned me with a look.

I smirked. "Okay, she's manipulative, but that's not changing."

"And you're allowing yourself to be manipulated which apparently isn't changing either." Gayle took a seat. "What's up with this Terrance anyway? You've never really talked about him before this. How do you feel about him?"

I let out a long breath and closed my eyes. "I don't know." I shook my head. "I haven't seen him in a few years. The last time I was home he was dating some woman from Atlanta, but that didn't work out."

"So, you keep up with his comings and goings."

"No, my sister gossips about everybody in Garrison. I listen."

"How do you feel when she talks about him?"

I shrugged. "Ambivalent. It's like I want him to move on, but I don't."

Gayle nodded. "I'm not trying to be a shrink here, but have you ever thought about why?"

I gave Gayle the stink eye. Yes, she was trying to play shrink. "Because he's the only man who has ever asked me to marry him. That's a big deal. It's like I want to keep him on a shelf for that."

Gayle looked confused. "I never wanted to keep anyone on a shelf."

I smirked again. "Gayle, you're gorgeous. You get a marriage proposal every day on the subway."

"From crazy men," she retorted.

"Well, you had four from men who weren't crazy before you finally accepted the fifth. Women like me don't have men falling all over us."

Gayle narrowed her glare. "What do you mean women like you?"

I wasn't sure what I meant. I let my words swirl around in my head before I responded. "Look, I know I'm pretty," I started. That was true, I wasn't as slim as I wanted to be, but my smooth mocha brown skin and large dark eyes had always been assets men complimented me on. Plus, I was a little on the tall side, five seven to be exact, my legs went on forever in the four inch heels I hiked around in everyday. Men couldn't seem to get enough of those either, but that had been in my twenties and early thirties. The catcalls were less frequent now and seemed to come from the mouths of drunks rather than good-looking men who were actually worth my time. The ones who weren't drunk were five foot five and balding. I sighed and waved my hand. "Let's move on."

Gayle slid a folder in front of me. "I did the things you asked. I reserved the banquet hall, the videographer and photographer. Those are the contracts from the vendors and your payment receipts. I'll email copies so you have digital copies."

"Fantastic. What would I do without you?"

"Hire two hardworking people to take my place." She chuckled. "I also have a call in to the D.J. and limousine company."

I sucked in a cleansing breath and fanned my fingers out across the desk. 'Great, that's a big help."

"Did you want me to get you a list of caterers?"

"Some back ups. I have a small company in town I'd like to use. I'm going to call them myself. They're family friends."

Gayle put the pen she'd borrowed back in my pencil holder. "Anything else?"

"Yes," I replied. "You can book me a flight to Atlanta. I'm headed to Garrison, Georgia, whether I want to or not."

Chapter 2

I hated flying, which was why I hadn't seen my sister since Christmas, nearly ten months ago. I stopped at a vending machine next to baggage claim, swiped my credit card and selected the ginger ale. Although I knew it didn't really have ginger in it, the soft drink had quelled my stomach from the time I was a young girl. A lifetime of bouts with motion sickness had sent my dad to the store on many occasions to get a bottle, so much so that he'd called me a "ginger-holic". I smiled at the thought and turned the top on the bottle. I took a long sip and washed down the pain of the memory of my dad. He'd been deceased five years and still the heartache from the loss hit me everyday.

"There you are." I heard Terrance's voice before I registered that it was him standing in front of me. Tall, dark and handsome. He was such a cliché.

"Terrance." That was all I could manage to say without wanting to scream.

He looked down at the floor like he was embarrassed and then raised his eyes to mine. I remembered the last time I'd really looked into his eyes. I wondered if he remembered.

"Sis!" Janette's shriek came from behind and startled me from my memory. She was quick for a pregnant woman. She closed the space between the ladies restroom and us within seconds. Her petite frame, five foot two in height, and never more than a size four was still as petite and cute as ever. It just had a huge lump protruding from it. The green monster that always reared his head when I thought about the favor my sister had in the figure department jumped on my shoulder. She would never be fat. Not even after having a baby.

Janette's chestnut brown skin glowed. Her dimples, the other thing I envied about my sister, framed her ridiculously gorgeous smile. A headband pushed her shoulder length strawberry blonde hair, likely a wig, off her face. I don't think I'd ever seen my sister with a headband on. She was already turning into a caricature of a housewife. She looked like a version of Reese Witherspoon dipped in chocolate for the newly filmed black version of *Sweet Home Alabama* staring, Beyoncé Knowles. She extended her arms. "I know I'm big as a house, but you can still get your arms around me."

I leaned down and squeezed. When I released her she scooted around me, grabbed Terrance's hand and said, "See honey, I told you she'd come."

"Was there any doubt?" I asked looking Terrance in the eyes again.

I watched his Adam's apple move up and down. He nodded. "Well, we all know Nectar hates planes, trains and automobiles."

Nectar, no he did not. I had to clench my fist to keep from clawing him.

"Darling." Janette grabbed his tie and gave it a good tug. "That little term of endearment you had for my sister has to go." She didn't look like Reese Witherspoon anymore. I'd never seen Reese roll her neck and snap her head back.

I sighed. This was exactly why you didn't get involved with a man someone you cared about had dated. You wouldn't have messy situations and messy words and messy emotions. I couldn't believe he'd just called me Nectar.

Terrance chuckled nervously and removed her hand from his tightly stretched neckwear. "Baby, you are going to choke me before I meet my son." He continued leaning his six foot towering body over to take Janette in his arms. "Besides, I've always called your sister Nectar and it was because she was always eating nectarines at lunch in school. You know that. I've been calling her Nectar since the first grade." He kissed Janette on the neck and continued to plant kisses behind her ear. "You are the only something sweet I'm going to want for the rest of my life."

Ugh, I wanted to turn around and get back on a plane to New York. They were making my sick stomach even sicker. No wonder she was pregnant. They needed to get a room.

I cleared my throat and put my carry-on down at their feet. "I'm going to find my luggage." Neither of them heard me. I departed anyway and located the carousel that indicated baggage for my flight from LaGuardia, New York. I pulled my lone bag off the conveyor belt and looked back at them. They were standing face to face, holding hands and chatting like the lovers they were. *Nectar.* Yes, he'd called me that for years, but it had special meaning when he whispered it in my ear the last time. It was on the night of my father's funeral. The night he'd discovered how sweet I really was. I groaned. This visit might be more difficult than I'd anticipated.

I removed my cell from my bag and sent a text to Gayle:

Tell me why I'm here again?

Less than sixty seconds passed and my answer came.

Because she's the only relative you care about. She's pregnant and she needs you. That's what you told me.

That was it. Our deceased parents would want me to support her, but they might have to do a visitation from heaven to help me make it through the next twelve days, because it was going to take an act of God to help me stop thinking about how I should have said yes when Terrance Wright proposed to me.

***

Garrison, Georgia was a different world from the hustle and bustle of Manhattan. I loved that Manhattan was a city that truly never slept and everything I wanted was within walking distance. Great shopping, cultural activities, a diverse offering of food including all the healthy choices I'd come to enjoy that had replaced soul food in my diet. But even with all that New York had to offer I did enjoy coming home from time to time for the peace and quiet and the occasional slab of sho' nuff fingerlickin' good southern barbeque. Licking ones fingers was not a cool thing to do in the city, but I could put my back into a meal in these parts. A girl needed to be able to do that once in a while.

We passed the sign alerting us to reduce our speed and Terrance let up on the accelerator. The road became two lanes, bordered on both sides by Japanese honeysuckles. The sweet scent of the flowers greeted us as we passed the "Welcome to Garrison" sign at the city's entrance.

Garrison was a small, quaint, town forty minutes outside of Atlanta. The downtown area was a roundabout filled with the city municipal buildings, shops, restaurants and a small cinema that played old movies that were on their last big screen before being packaged on DVD and placed in the *Red Box*. There were a few homes and rooming houses in town, but the majority of residents lived outside of the circle in the houses and subdivisions that encompassed an eighteen square mile area. Like the rest of Georgia, it was segregated, the whites living on the west half of the circle, blacks living on the east and the growing Latino population fitting in wherever they could. Like many small towns across the United States, it had taken a hit during the recession. A few storefronts were boarded up and some of the buildings needed a fresh coat of paint, including the city municipal building.

"Can you believe they're holding a fundraiser to buy

paint and bricks to resurface the court house?" Terrance asked like he'd been reading my mind. "The city is just that broke." Those were the first words he'd said since he'd spoken at the airport. I almost welcomed the sound of his voice, because Janette hadn't stopped yakking since we'd piled into Terrance's truck.

I was seated in the rear of course, and listened while my sister rattled on and on about what she really wanted to get off her wedding registry and how she hoped her friends would still have money to buy a gift off her baby registry. She also talked about all the things she wanted in the wedding. As far as I could tell, she didn't have the money or the time for most of it. From the side view, I could see Terrance grimacing every time she mentioned something that sounded the least bit expensive. I wondered if he had funds to help pull this event off or if I was expected to not only suffer through the planning and execution, but also finance it. I sighed. I knew my sister was broke. I sent her money every month.

Terrance stopped the truck in front of our family home. Like many of the houses it had been built to accommodate the warm, humid climate and included a large wrap-around porch that provided shade during the heat of the day. The roof was pitched with dormers and it was white wood that appeared to have recently been painted. I couldn't help but think of my parents every time I saw it, especially my father. He took such pride in owning this house and was meticulous about its upkeep.

"I put a coat of paint on it back in the spring. I know how your Dad was about touching it up, even when it wasn't quite necessary," Terrance said as if he'd been reading my mind again. I didn't respond. Although I appreciated it, I figured paint was the least Terrance could do for my father, after-all, he'd knocked up his baby daughter.

The door opened to my right and Terrance extended a

hand to help me climb down. I felt a jolt of electricity ignite and race through my body when he touched me. He fought to look anywhere but at me and then finally did when both my feet were on the ground.

"This is wrong," I said. "I shouldn't be here."

Terrance swallowed and turned my hand loose. "I'll get your bags." He made his escape.

"Niecy, what do you think of my flowers?" Janette had her back to us. She had already traveled along the walkway a bit. She stood there with her hands on her hips. From the rear you couldn't even tell she was pregnant. Her video girl booty was still sitting just as high as it always had. As I closed the space between us, my thoughts flashed back in time to a memory of my mother sitting on that porch. I had only been five when she was killed in a car accident. I didn't remember much about her, but I remember her sitting on the porch in a rocking chair braiding my hair and humming hymns from church.

The scent of sweet olive flowers drifted to my nose from the planters on both sides of the porch. This house was my parent's legacy. It made me remember why I was actually here. Family. Promises. I was here to be a sister even if I'd been betrayed by my own.

"It's beautiful," I replied.

Janette wrapped her arm around mine and leaned her head onto my shoulder like she'd always done when we were kids. "I'm so glad you're here. I'm so glad I'm not alone in the world," she said and I thought she had read my mind.

"I'll stick your luggage on the porch and be going." Terrance passed us and put my suitcases at the top of the steps. He walked back toward us and leaned in to give Janette a quick peck on the cheek. "Call me later," was all he said and within moments the truck he'd never turned off was in gear and moving down the road.

Janette released my arm. "Come on. Let's go in. We have a lot to talk about, but your nephew is sitting on my bladder. I've got to pee."

***

By seven p.m. that evening the living room was filled with women that Janette and I had grown up with. Terrance's mother, whom I'd affectionately always known as Mother Wright and his sister, Pamela, a girl I'd never liked and now a woman I couldn't stand, were also present for the planning of the whirlwind nuptials. I didn't need this many hands. In fact, I didn't need any of them except on the day of the reception to decorate, but this party had been set prior to my arrival. The good news was it was a potluck meeting so the table was covered with enough casseroles, meat dishes and desserts to keep Janette and I fed until we sat down for the rehearsal dinner.

A few big things had already been done. The wedding invitations had gone out weeks ago. The location of the ceremony was easy…Terrance's father's church. Mount Moriah Christian Church had beautiful grounds and a gorgeous gazebo and pond behind it. It was the perfect backdrop for a country wedding and the pictures. If it had been spring or summer I'd have planned an outside event, but it was mid October and the weather, although arid today, could be unpredictably chilly for outdoors. We decided to have the ceremony inside. Gayle reserved a local banquet hall for the reception.

"How many people are in the wedding party?" I asked. Janette had originally selected twelve women but I'd told her it was way too many. They were only expecting a hundred or so guests. You couldn't have twelve attendants when you only had a hundred people. If I was planning this wedding, she wasn't going to mess with my sensibilities and break all the wedding rules.

Four women and Pamela raised their hands.

"And then there's you," Janette added.

"Janette, I've already told you I can't be in the wedding. I'm coordinating the event."

"No need for that." Mother Wright stood to her feet. "We have a coordinator. Sister Marie does it all the time and she's really very good."

Good compared to whom, I thought, but I merely nodded. The look in Mother Wright's eyes was one that chastised me. She shook her head as if to say, "*You are not going to get out of standing up for your sister.*" I got the message.

"Mother is right. Sister Marie can direct everyone in," Janette said. "You must be my maid of honor. You're my sister after all. You can't *not* be in my wedding."

A loud harrumph came from Janette's right. "She can pass if she wants to. I wouldn't be in no wedding if my sister was marrying my ex-boyfriend," Pamela stated. "As a matter of fact, I wouldn't even be in town that day."

The room fell silent. All eyes were on me including Mother Wright's. They were waiting for what I'd have to say about that.

Janette stood to her feet, supported her weight by placing her hand near the small of her back and wobbled her way toward me. I noticed she wobbled a whole lot more when Terrance wasn't around. She moaned and groaned a bit too. She'd been working hard to look cute in front of her fiancé, which was so typical of my sister. Never let a man see you sweat. That was her motto.

"Now, we're not going to talk about Niecy's old relationship with Terrance. That's been over. They are both over each other. My sister loves me. We have her blessing to get married. Don't we Niece?"

I swallowed hard and lifted my glass of ice tea and took a sip. I nodded and repeated the lines I could completely agree with. "Terrance and I have been over. I love my sister."

I wasn't as convincing as I'd hoped I'd be. A few eyes rolled and some heads shook. You could hear a pin drop until Mother Wright clapped her hands and said, "Let's get back to what we came here for. Next on the list is the food for the rehearsal dinner, right?" She encouraged me with a close-lipped smile and a nod of her head. I had never been really close to Mother Wright, but I knew the kind of woman she was. She cared about family. It meant everything to her. She was probably the only person in the room who really knew why I was here. No matter what I felt about it all, Janette was my sister. I had to get over the betrayal of the marriage and fight for the relationship that our deceased parents would want us to have, no matter what my sister had chosen to do to splinter it.

"Yes." I fought against gritting my teeth. "Let's talk about the menu."

By ten p.m. the house was empty, the food put away and my sister was in bed sleeping with her mouth open like she'd picked cotton all day. She was still in the bedroom she'd grown up in, refusing to move into the master where my father had taken his last breath during hospice. I understood that. I couldn't bring myself to sleep in the room either. It was a shrine to our parents and we wordlessly agreed to let it stay that way.

Unlike Janette, I wasn't tired. Even after the flight and ride from the airport and the fight to keep my emotions in check, I was still a bit wired and unable to sleep. I'd forgotten how quiet it was here. The Upper West side of Manhattan had the undercurrent of city noise twenty-four hours a day. I wasn't used to the silence. After an unsuccessful attempt to watch television and read a novel, I grabbed my sister's keys, locked the house up and climbed into her car. I didn't drive very often. I didn't have a car. I'd purposely chosen to live where I could use other means of transportation, because having a car in the city was a burden. I took taxicabs wherever I had to go from the upper west side to the lower east side. And if I was desperate, the subway system would do.

I sucked in a deep breath to quell the nausea that always kind of engulfed me when I sat behind the wheel of a car, started it and pulled out of the driveway onto the main road. I turned on the radio. Music from the Quiet Storm crooned through the speakers. This radio station probably wasn't the right choice as the romantic love songs only served to remind me of what I'd been fighting to forget all day, really, all month…that no one loved me. I was thirty-six years old, hadn't had a date in over six months and now the only man that had ever really wanted me was marrying my sister. I pulled the car over to the side of the road and burst into tears.

"Durn you, Janette, you could have had anyone. Why Terrance?" I cried and I cried and I cried. I was crying so hard that I hadn't even noticed a car had stopped behind me until I heard the light rap on the passenger side window. My heart froze with fear. Had I checked all my city slickness with my bag at the airport? What was I doing sitting on the side of the road in a car at eleven p.m. in the country? Waiting for a serial killer? I took the car out of park. I let it leap forward a bit to signal him to get out of the way before he was in the ditch. The only reason I didn't gun the engine was because I might have dragged him down the road.

"Nectar! Wait! It's me."

Nectar, nobody called me that but…I put my foot on the brake and leaned a bit to my right to get a better look at him. Well, there was one other person who called me by that silly nickname. I pushed the button to let the window down. "Ethan Wright?!!"

Chapter 3

Ethan was Terrance's first cousin on his father's side. He'd been abandoned by his mother when he was eight and had come to live with Pastor and Mother Wright. His mother was said to be a weed smokin' hippie who had run off with a boyfriend to backpack her way across the country. She'd never come "right back" for Ethan as she'd promised. Sadly, she'd been brought back to Garrison in a casket when he was thirteen. The rumor was that she'd died from a drug overdose. Terrance had shared that Ethan's father was unknown. It was very sad.

However, early tragedy aside, Ethan was Garrison's biggest success story. A star athlete who'd gone all the way from middle school soccer to play in college and then professionally for over five years in Europe until his knee was injured, at which point he retired. His career ended on a high. He banged up his knee earning the final winning point in the World Cup.

"When I first saw the car on the side of the road I thought you were Janette. I thought her car had broken down." Ethan slid a glass of water across the granite countertop in his enormous, modern and breathtakingly beautiful kitchen.

"Well, I'm neither," I replied, taking a sip from the glass. "I thought you were Ted Bundy or his twisted cousin."

He smiled, shrugged and raised a glass to his lips. "I'm neither either."

Good Lord, I thought. That was a nice smile. When we were growing up he had kinks and curls that would make most naturally curly girls green with envy, but for whatever reason he was sporting a shaved head. A five o'clock shadow framed his chin and tried as I might to ignore it, I could see a fine curly mass of hair twisting its way from under his shirt. His skin was sun-kissed a shade darker than its normal chocolate brown.

I hadn't seen Ethan since my father's funeral. Although he'd been only about twenty-four at the time, I remembered thinking how incredibly handsome he'd grown to be, but now at twenty-nine leaning against the counter in his kitchen wearing a pair of low slung jeans and a muscle shirt he was down right FINE! Terrance's younger cousin had definitely grown up. All the way up. He wasn't looking like anybody's younger anything. He was holding it down as his own man.

I cleared my throat to clear my head. "Thanks for stopping. That was considerate."

"This is Garrison. I don't think anybody would have passed you by."

I nodded. He was right. In small towns everyone was friendly and considerate about things like breakdowns, because everyone acknowledged that if you could give the time of day to a dog, you could certainly give it to your neighbor. That was so unlike New York. I'd have waited five hours for a tow truck and then the driver would have been rude.

"What are you doing here?" I asked.

"I, uh, own this house," the smart aleck replied, smiling again.

"I know that, but the wedding's not for more than a week. You're a bit early to be in town. I thought you were in Africa, or something, building wells or houses for Habitat for Humanity."

"I was, but I'm in the middle of some business and it's local. I've been in Garrison for a while."

I nodded. "Local business. I can't imagine anything

around here that would hold your interest."

He took another sip of water. "You'd be surprised at what holds my interest." The look in his eyes was salacious. He was flirting.

My mouth curved into a smile. I had not expected that, so it was time to move on to another topic. "I've never been in this house." I stood and walked back into the living room. I could hear him follow.

"You want a tour? I completely remodeled it. It's not the house my grandfather owned."

I could see that. The floor to ceiling glass windows, marble floors and countertops were definitely not the materials any house in Garrison had when his grandfather was alive.

"Not tonight." I stopped in front of his piano. It was a beautiful ebony wood with a glossy polish. "You play?"

He nodded and pushed himself off the wall he'd momentarily stopped to lean against. "You wanna hear?" He'd closed the distance between us. His closeness threw heat in my direction that the large, leaf shaped, ceiling fan couldn't cool.

"It's late. I should be getting back. Janette might wake up and find me gone. I walked out without my cell and I didn't leave a note." I was talking too quickly. I sounded like a schoolgirl instead of a mature woman.

"It'll only take a minute for me to serenade you." He took my hand and pulled me with him onto the seat. Then he pushed the lid up and began playing chopsticks.

I had been taut as a rubber band. Sitting next to all those manly biceps and triceps had unnerved me a bit. Plus, he smelled as sexy as the men's cologne counter at Macys, but now I laughed and it was amazing how much tension I'd just released. "You're silly."

He chuckled and it was a deep sexy sound that reminded me how long it had been since I'd sat with a man that wasn't somebody's groom.

"No, for real, I wanted to make you laugh." He turned his face toward me. I tried to look straight ahead, but I couldn't. I knew he was waiting for me to meet his gaze. "You needed that laugh."

Ethan returned his long, handsome fingers to the delicate ivory keys and after a few seconds I recognized the tune he was playing as "Ribbon in the Sky". After he played a little of the song he began to sing. "Oh so long for this night I prayed."

"Wow, Ethan. I didn't know you —"

He raised a hand against my interruption and continued to sing for the next few minutes until he completed the song.

I was impressed and overcome with all kinds of emotion. I'd never had a man play the piano for me unless he was auditioning for a wedding and I definitely hadn't had anyone sing in such a sexy timbre. I couldn't believe he had such a beautiful voice and could play so perfectly. He took my hand and continued in acapella. "If allowed, may I touch your hand..."

I'd been staring straight ahead, but now I turned toward him and looked into those amazing limpid pools God had given him for eyes. The room shrank. The oxygen disappeared. He leaned forward and kissed me. It started off gentle and easy, just two people exploring the outside of each others lips with smooches, but then he raised his hand to my chin and whispered, "Open your mouth."

I did as I was told. The sensation that erupted from our tongues touching caused blood to shoot to all kinds of places on my body. I gasped and pulled back, shook my head. "No, this is wrong." I slid from behind the bench and stood.

Ethan shrugged. He didn't look surprised. He didn't even look disappointed.

"I'm going to go." I looked around for my purse, but then realized I left it at the house. All I had were the keys in my pocket. "Janette might be out of her mind with worry."

"Is that really why you're leaving?"

"What?" I asked as if I hadn't heard him.

"Never mind." He waved my question off and closed the lid on the keyboard. "Speaking of Janette, before you go, let's get back to those tears I witnessed. Are you alright?"

I was hoping he wouldn't bring that up. I was embarrassed enough as it was that he'd seen me wailing by the side of the road like a lovesick puppy. "I'm fine."

"You didn't look fine."

"Well, I'm fine now." I wasn't really and it had nothing to do with my crying. He'd kissed me. He seemed totally unaffected by it. I was still trying to get my head together.

Ethan paused as if considering my response and then said, "I could make you feel lots better."

I cocked my head back. "What exactly do you mean by that?"

"You want the clean version?"

I pursed my lips. "Definitely."

"Suit yourself." He smiled devilishly. "Actually, I only have a clean version. I'd never disrespect you with any other." His smile continued to contradict his words. "I was thinking we could hang out while you're in town. You know since you came in so early too."

"I'll be busy. I'm planning the wedding." I squared my shoulders, preparing for what I knew was coming.

Ethan stood to his feet, leaned forward and put a finger

behind his ear. "Come again."

"I said I'll be busy organizing the wedding."

Ethan whistled and stuck his fists in his pockets, which caused his jeans to ride even lower across his unbelted hips. "I mean, why would you do that?"

"I'm a wedding planner. That's what I do for a living."

"And?"

"And she needed my help. You have to have a professional if you want things to go smoothly, especially at this late date."

Ethan chuckled. "You should be kidding."

"I'm not."

"I know you're not that's why I said should. Why would you put yourself through that?"

"It's not a big deal. It's actually a good thing. It'll keep me busy."

"A good thing. Your sister is marrying your ex."

I cocked my head to the side. "You don't have to tell me that. I'm well aware of it."

"So, because you're a wedding planner that means you have to plan their ridiculous wedding? I don't think so." Ethan was making sense. Of course, to someone on the outside looking in, it seemed a simple choice for me. Pass on the planning, pass on the wedding if I wanted, but it wasn't, not for me.

"Because, I'm her sister. People would expect me to do it."

"Forget people," Ethan angled his head. "What about you?"

"I'll be fine." My tone was resolute and I thought

convincing.

"Bull, they should have protected you from this. They should have eloped. Not like they don't have a reason to."

Not wanting to continue the debate I shook my head. "Ethan, this isn't a big deal."

"Need I remind you that you were crying on the side of the road less than an hour ago?"

"I wasn't crying because of that," I said raising my voice a bit.

He was unconvinced. The expression on his face said so before his words confirmed it. "Oh, really?"

"I wasn't crying because of the wedding. Have you ever thought that the reason I was crying might be private? That I don't want to talk about it. That I don't want to share."

He shook his head. "I'm sorry, I thought you women liked to talk out stuff."

"And I'm sure you're an expert on us women."

He crossed his arms over his chest and cocked his head. "Now who's making assumptions?"

"I'm not assuming. You've already proven yourself to be slick with your singing and piano playing."

He chuckled and dropped his arms. Well-chiseled biceps tightened and distracted me for a moment. "You asked me about the piano."

I raised my eyebrows a fraction. "I didn't ask you to play and I certainly didn't ask you to sing."

He shook his head again. "I'm sorry. I just wanted to take your mind off your troubles. You seemed to need some help with that."

"Yeah, I'm sure that's what the kiss was for too."

"No." He rubbed his head and smiled, devilishly. "The kiss was purely selfish."

Our eyes locked and words escaped us. I was the first to break the stare. "I'm going." I turned and headed toward the door.

"Wait up. I'll follow you."

I turned the knob and pulled the door open. "There's no need. I know the way home."

He closed the space between us and pulled on the sneakers he'd taken off when we entered the house. "No way are you going out of here this late alone. I'm following you to make sure you get in the house."

I couldn't talk him out if it. He did just that, followed me to the house, waited for me to get out and inside and then he pulled off.

I closed the door and leaned against it. I felt like a fool yet again. Not only were Janette and Terrance making a fool out of me, but now I'd made a fool out of myself running away from a kiss like I was a sixteen-year-old schoolgirl. I raised my hands to my lips, remembered the feel of his lips against mine.

"Open your mouth." O.M.G. I closed my eyes against the memory. That Ethan Wright was sexy and I loved a man that knew how to take control. I let out a long sigh. "Get it together girl. You're vulnerable and you did not come to town to be some man with wanderlust in his blood's booty call."

I flopped down on the sofa. Gayle was probably still up, although likely watching a movie with her new husband. They did that every Sunday night. So, instead of calling like I wanted to I sent a text.

Me: *Today was interesting. Hated seeing Terrance. Couldn't help but love seeing my sister. She's cute pregnant. Met up with Terrance's cousin, Ethan.*

Gayle: *Ethan Wright, that fine soccer player?*

Me: *Ex-soccer player. Fine is an understatement. I just left his house.*

Gayle didn't send her message back as quickly as she usually did. I wondered if she'd drifted off the sleep or decided to do what married people did and then a message came through.

Gayle: *His house huh? Watch it, Diva. You're vulnerable right now. Be careful not to do the wrong thing with another Mr. Wright.*

I sighed and tossed my phone across the sofa.

Chapter 4

My sister had selected a white wedding dress. She was getting married in a church to the pastor's son, so it was not the color I would have selected. I couldn't talk her out of it. I put my wedding planner sensibilities in the back of my mind and recalled the advice I always gave my clients when they were unsure about a choice they were making for their wedding: "Etiquette may dictate certain rules, but this is your day. Make it what you want it to be." My sister deserved the same pass on her white dress.

"You look amazing." I took her hand.

She seemed uncertain and so tiny, even with the bulge in front of her. "I'm so glad you're here. I couldn't do this without you. Are you sure I don't look too fat? Too pregnant?"

The only way she was hiding that belly was under a garbage can, but the dress she'd chosen, an empire cut with the large voile and lace sash below the breast line with a free flowing skirt, was a good start. "You look beautiful and since we're only a little over a week out, you don't have to worry about out growing it."

Janette grunted a bit. "I guess not. I just want everything to be perfect. It's bad enough daddy isn't here to walk me down the aisle. I don't want anything else making me sad."

I nodded. I understood exactly what she meant. I'd thought about it myself on many occasions as I instructed a father to cup the elbow of his daughter and take that long walk to hand her off to her future husband. I'd wondered who would do that for me.

"Now that we're on that subject who is it that has the honor of giving you away?"

Janette walked across the room and reached into a tissue box to remove one. "Uncle Murray." She dabbed at the moisture that had pooled around her eyes. "Who else?"

I nodded. Randolph Murray or Uncle Murray, as we called him, wasn't our actual uncle. We didn't have any uncles. Both our parents had been only children; hence our tiny circle of family. He was Janette's godfather and had been our father's best friend. He'd adored her since she was a little girl.

"I'd better get out of this dress. I don't want the other girls to see it."

She entered the dressing room just as the bell over the door to the small shop rang and in came the group of other bridesmaids. We'd already discussed the fact that we had to take something that the shop owner had on the rack. The only dress that had been picked out prior to my arrival was Janette's and she and I had done the shopping using FaceTime on our iPhones. As for the wedding party, she insisted the girls wait for me to come to town so whatever they selected wouldn't clash with my vision. Thankfully none of the girls were particularly small or large, so the store's stock would be sufficient.

Evie, the shop owner, had agreed to get started on alternations immediately so we could come back in a few days for the fittings and still have time for one more if necessary.

Janette wanted everyone to wear hot pink, so we selected fuchsia dresses that were on consignment from a summer wedding that had been cancelled. Lucky for us, not so lucky for the couple I supposed. In any event, fuchsia was my sister's favorite color and she was tickled pink that everyone was able to fit in one of the dresses. There was even a dress for the flower girl available. Terrance's cousin would be coming in after school to try it on, but based on the size and save for a little hemming, we were certain it would fit the child.

Janette, complaining of back pain, hugged everyone and made her exit to the car to wait for me. I stayed behind to pay for mine and the other dresses that weren't in the last minute budgets for two of Janette's friends. They both thanked me profusely and insisted they would pay me back, but I told them I was Janette's family. I was standing in my dad's place therefore I'd take care of it. As they would say in Garrison, I made a heap more money than she did. I didn't want her trying to take a mortgage on the house to pay for a wedding, which was what she had a mind to do.

Renea, Janette's best friend, and I were the last in the shop. We'd agreed to a secret lunch meeting to discuss the bridal shower, which Renea had already told me she had huge ideas for. I would have loved handing off the shower in its entirety. But I sensed budget was an issue, so rather than dump it all on her, I agreed to be part of the planning. I honestly understood budgetary issues. A wedding in thirty days could be a burden on anyone. It did my heart good to see that my sister had done such a great job holding on to her high school friends, because I hadn't. I'd been so busy working that I didn't even really talk to anyone from college forget high school.

The next stop on our list was the local bakery. It was a delicious little shop owned by Ward Simpson, a member of Reverend Wright's church and had been in the owner's family for nearly seventy years. We tasted samples of his lemon, raspberry and coconut cream fillings and settled on a plain white velvet cake with a seedless raspberry filling. I had my own plans for how to decorate it, so that made the short delivery window a non-issue. I told Mr. Simpson Terrance would be popping in later today to select a groom's cake and I had no idea what he had in mind.

"Knowing Terrance it won't be anything too crazy," Mr. Simpson replied. He handed me the receipt for the cake and a bag that included two complimentary cupcakes for Janette and me. My sister took the bag and started waddling out the door to the car, pleading the need to sit down again.

"I'll be back in later to order the bridal shower cake," I whispered. Mr. Simpson winked like we were keeping a huge secret and I followed Janette to the car.

I no longer needed my sister, so I dropped her off at work. The tuxedo shop was next on my list. I was meeting with Terrance and his groomsmen. I was pleased to see that the shop had a nice selection of tuxedos that could be ordered quickly. The men had to pay a twenty-dollar rush fee for the short window, but that didn't seem to be an issue for any of them and if it were, that would be Terrance's bill. The bell over the door rang and I turned expecting to see Terrance enter, but was surprised that it was Ethan.

He spotted me right away, removed the mirrored sunglasses he'd been wearing and made a slow, sexy approach. The sexiness wasn't on purpose. Ethan just had natural swagger.

"I didn't know you were in the wedding. Why didn't you tell me?"

"Good morning to you too," he replied.

I rolled my eyes. "Sorry, is it just morning? I've already had a full day. How are you?"

"I'm great. I had a good nights sleep. Dreamt of you the entire time."

The smile I'd had on my face dropped. I could see the flirting wasn't going to end with this guy. "So, back to my question, why didn't you tell me you were in the wedding?"

"I'm his first cousin," Ethan said, moving a few tuxedos around on the rack. He removed a really hideous one that looked more like a clown suit, frowned and returned it to the rack. "Why wouldn't I be in his wedding?" Ethan continued.

"Not only am I in the wedding, but I've been upgraded. Terrance called me this morning and promoted me up the ranks. You remember Craig Bond, his best friend?"

I nodded that I did.

"His unit has new orders. He's being deployed on Tuesday."

I was sorry for Craig for a moment, but then realized if Craig was out… "Does that mean you're going to be his best man?"

"Yeah, ironic right? We could barely stand each other growing up."

The bell over the shop rang again. Terrance and his friends entered with Uncle Murray on their heels.

"Childhood rivalries are often put aside for weddings," I said. "Let's join them."

A devilish look crossed Ethan's face. "Let's drop down to the floor, hide between the racks and pretend we're not here."

I leaned into him. "You are really silly."

"Ethan. Nec… Deniece," Terrance corrected himself. "I see you've become reacquainted."

"No reacquainting needed." Ethan put his arm around my shoulder. "Who could forget a gal like Deniece or a dude like me?"

The smile Terrance had on his face was replaced with a look of annoyance. I didn't miss the fact that he'd seemed particularly perturbed that Ethan had an arm around my shoulder.

I stepped out of Ethan's grasp and pinned him with a look that said, "Stop misbehaving," and slid into Uncle Murray's waiting arms for a hug.

"You're a good girl, Deniece. Your father would be proud of you." Uncle Murray gave my shoulder a comforting pat and winked. Like most folks in town, he knew that Terrance and I had been a couple. I appreciated the fact that he understood my showing up and helping my sister was about my father. If it hadn't been for the promise I made to him I might be in my condo eating a quart of ice cream and feeling sorry for myself.

"Is everyone here?" I asked Terrance.

Still a bit salty, he gave his head a curt nod.

"Great." There was no need to corral the men like I'd had to do with the women. They weren't the least bit distracted by the trappings in the store, so I was able to get right to it. "Good morning, gentleman. I think I know everyone from high school. If you don't remember me, I'm Deniece Malcolm. I'm the wedding planner and I'll be helping you with the tuxedo selection today."

They nodded and we started shopping. Getting the men fitted was as easy as finding pork at the Piggly Wiggly. Groomsmen were usually easy to please. They accepted my recommendation as fashion gospel and we matched the colors for their accessories with ease.

Evie, doing double duty in this store, which adjoined her dress shop, measured them, took payments and had them on their way in less than two hours. That left Ethan, Terrance and me at the counter.

Terrance stepped to the register to pay for his tuxedo and Ethan turned to me. "Would you like to have lunch? I promise. They'll be no piano music or singing."

I smiled. "I liked your playing and it's a tempting offer, but I have a bridal shower party to plan, so I'm busy for lunch."

He nodded understanding, but didn't give up. "Dinner?"

I squinted and remembered what he'd said last night about us hanging out. I also remembered that kiss that felt so right, but was obviously very wrong. "I don't know. My to-do list is pretty long and I should spend some time with Janette."

"Janette's going to Bible study tonight. She goes every week. She is marrying the Reverend's son you know." Ethan winked at me.

"What was that about the reverend's son?" Terrance interrupted, suspicion tinged his tone.

"Deniece was agreeing to have dinner with me since Janette will be at Bible study."

"Dinner?" Terrance didn't hide his surprise. "With you?"

Ethan put his arms around my shoulder again. "Nectar and I hung out last night, but we have some more catching up to do."

I moved from under his suggestive arm.

"More." Terrance's tone was grumpy. "She doesn't like to be called Nectar anymore."

I rolled my eyes. He was clueless. "I asked you not to call me that."

Terrance's face twisted in pain, but he nodded agreeably. "I'm not going to Bible study this evening, because I have to work late. I was hoping you and I could meet and talk."

I shook my head. "Anything you have to say to me you can say at the house when Janette's there."

"I'd rather not," he continued.

I shook my head again. "Please, don't try to…" I paused not sure even what I wanted to say. "You and I had our say years ago. There's nothing else to be said and besides, I'm having dinner with Ethan. I've already accepted."

"Tomorrow then," Terrance pleaded.

"She'll probably want to have dinner with me again," Ethan winked at him. "I'm that dude."

Terrance was incensed.

I cast a frustrated glance between the two of them. "I don't have time for this. Ethan, six is good for me. Terrance, please don't forget to go to the bakery and order your grooms cake. They're expecting you."

"I'm on my way there now—"

His words were in the wind. I exited the shop without giving either one of them a goodbye and climbed in the car before they could stop me. I wasn't about to be in the middle of their pissing contest. Terrence had a lot of nerve flexing his ego.

I made a stop at the florist and picked up the wedding price list. I figured I could study it after lunch and then stop back by to place the order. Janette had already told me she trusted me to make that call. She'd seen enough pictures from my events to know that I had a knack for making the right selections.

I had to wait a few minutes for Renea because she was late. I was trying to focus on the flowers, but couldn't really get my mind off of what had happened back at the tuxedo shop. Terrance did not like that last comment Ethan had made and it troubled me as to why. I hadn't planned on spending five minutes alone with him while I was in town. I hadn't planned on allowing him the satisfaction of giving me his sorry excuse for why he'd dined, bedded, and knocked up my sister, but now seeing how crazy he'd looked when Ethan told him about our date I thought I might have to give him that five minutes after all. I needed to know where his head was and more importantly if his heart was in the right place.

A bell rang over the door. Every shop and restaurant in Garrison had one and I turned to see Renea hustling to the table.

"Sorry I'm late. I had two heads with relaxer on them." She slid onto the chair opposite me. "I had to get those ladies under the dryer before I left and I had to make up an excuse that didn't make your sister suspicious."

"It's okay. I had plenty to think about while I waited." I picked up the menu.

"Speaking of relaxers, were you going to need me to do your hair before the wedding?"

I touched my freshly washed and styled twist-out. Was she kidding? "No, I do my own hair, thanks."

"It's just that Janette said something about wanting all the girls to have the same hairstyle."

"I've been able to do a lot for my sister in the last month, but straightening my hair isn't going to be one of them."

"You said a mouth full. You've been really good about this wedding." Renea emphasized the word good.

"That's not a hard thing to do. My relationship with Terrance ended a long time ago." I sounded convincing, even to myself.

"Yeah, but still there's the ex-factor. You know sisters don't date each others exes," Renea said, putting the undeniable truth on the table.

"It's probably a really silly rule," I continued to attempt to save face. "Especially since there's a shortage of good men. A woman could be missing out on a great guy." I reached for my water glass and took a sip. I hid behind it, just like I was hiding behind the words I'd said, as if I actually believed the lies that were coming out of my own mouth.

"Whatever, I would have an issue with it. Now he's dated you both. Is he comparing?"

Heat rose to my face and I returned my glass to the table. "I don't think men are that deep."

"It would still bother me. But it's obvious it doesn't bother you and that's great for everyone involved I suppose." Renea yawned and stretched her hand over her head like my refusal to be messy about it was boring her.

The waitress arrived at our table. We ordered sandwiches and iced tea and she sashayed away promising to be back in a jiffy. I decided to head Renea off. "No more talk about the ex-factor. Let's get to this party."

"That's fine by me," Renea said. "I have a great idea for the party. I think we should have it at that new fancy place over on Pine Road. It's called Palermo's. It's a restaurant that serves Toughen Italian food."

"Toughen," I repeated and then realization dawned on me. "Tuscan."

"What?"

"Tuscany is a part of Italy. That's why they call it Tuscan food."

Renea nodded. "Oh. Okay. I get that. Anyway," she continued, "people are talking about it like it's the best thing since sweetwater cornbread. The décor is really nice and you need a reservation on weekends. People come all the way from Atlanta and Alabama to eat there."

Folks were traveling to this place. I heard a cash register cha-ching in my head. "I assumed we'd have the party at someone's house."

"Well we could, but I ain't got time to clean mine up and the other girls don't think their houses are nice enough."

"Our house is fine."

"But how are we going to surprise her at her own house? I think Palermo's should be good, if they have space. You'll find that out won't you?"

What she meant was, I'd find out what the space cost. I merely nodded.

"I don't think we should have a stripper or anything." Renea raised a hand to the side of her face and whispered. "First Lady Wright is probably going to come."

I propped my chin on my fist. "She'll come if she's invited. She doesn't have to be you know and the party doesn't really have to be surprise."

Renea twisted her lip like she'd never considered either possibility. "Well, we can't have a stripper at the restaurant, so… let's just stick to a nice dinner in a private room with gifts and games and pictures. That seems more appropriate for a pregnant bride don't you think?"

I relented. "I'll check on Palermo's."

Renea clapped her hands gleefully. "As soon as you let me know about it, I'll call the girls. Can you see if they have this Sunday afternoon? I think a Sunday afternoon is best."

The waitress returned with our meals. Renea inhaled her sandwich and sucked down her tea in what seemed like one large slurp. She reached into her purse and exclaimed. "I forgot my wallet at the shop. I had to get change out for a customer."

"No problem. I have it." *It's nothing compared to the meal you want me to pay for at Palermo's,* I thought.

"Great. I need to get back to the shop. Text me and let me know the details." She stood and gave me a hug. "Good luck with the rest of your planning stuff."

I sat back in my chair. Good luck was right. I had way

too many things to do and had yet to decide what we would do for decorations and favors. I wished I'd had time to order those from my favorite little place in North Carolina, but I didn't. They required too much notice and I hadn't given any real thought to what I would do for Janette prior to getting on the plane. This was just not my favorite wedding to plan.

The bell rang over the restaurant door and in sauntered Ethan. I was beginning to think he was following me and I intended to tell him so. He spotted me right away and made his way to my table. "Fancy finding you here."

"I was wondering if I needed a restraining order."

Ethan laughed and dropped his body into the chair Renea had vacated. "No need for that, Luv. I only stay where I'm wanted."

I guffawed. "So I guess you'll be rising from that seat soon."

He threw his hands up. "You're snarky. What's gotten into you?"

I sighed and dropped my head in my hands for a moment. I raised my head and met his eyes. Ethan had the sexist eyes I had ever seen in my life. They were downright dreamy and always looked like he'd just woken up. That was the hotness.

"You don't want to know because you already think I'm being silly."

"You can't get sillier." He chuckled, but then raised his hands in surrender, "I digress. I won't mention that again."

The waitress approached our table and hands on hips, breast "up and at'em" she stood right in front of Ethan. She was so close that he could have licked her if he stuck his tongue out. "You want the usual?" she asked twisting a lock of her needed to be tightened weave around her finger.

"Yes, ma'am. Extra fries please. I'm hungry today."

She blushed and switched her big behind away from the table. Ethan spared me the agony of watching her move that thing by keeping his eyes on me.

"See, I told you I wasn't stalking. I've been eating here every day since I came home."

I grunted. Surprised it bothered me so that someone was coming on to him.

"And how long has that been?"

"Nearly a month," he replied. "But forget about me. I want to know what's eating you." He took my hand in his and played with my fingers. His touch burned…sizzled. I couldn't remember the last time a man touched my hand so intimately.

I cleared my throat. "It's everything. The time, the cost…not that I don't have the money, but I don't know it just weird that everyone would presume that I should pay for everything. Where's Terrance's money?"

Ethan let my hand go and threw his back against the chair. "Tied up right now. He's in the middle of a business deal and trust me, he is capital strapped."

I remembered why Ethan said he was in town. "Is it the same business you're here for?"

He nodded. "I'll let you in on a little secret, but you have to promise not to tell Janette."

I nodded agreement.

"Terrance went on that reality T.V. show called Investment Bank a few months ago. He didn't get a deal with one of the investors, but I and a few other folks I know thought it was a good idea, so we've put some money up."

"Seriously."

He nodded. "Janette doesn't even know he did the show. It's a surprise. It'll air in a few weeks."

"Interesting," I said, thinking about how much my sister loved reality television shows. "So, if it's such a good idea why didn't the investors on the show go for it?"

"He said he didn't do a good job with the numbers."

I raised a curious eyebrow. "The numbers aren't good, but you're helping him anyway?"

"The numbers are great. He just flubbed the presentation. You know how Terrance gets when he's nervous." Ethan frowned. "Anyway, I managed to get a few buddies to go in with me. We're in for over a half a million dollars."

"Over half a mil? I knew you soccer players made good money, but that's a lot to invest in a new business."

"It's a good business and besides, it's just sitting in the bank. He needed it. Why not?"

"Because, as you said this morning you guys never seemed to like each other."

Ethan shrugged. "We're family. We don't have to like each other that much to go into business together. I can trust him."

I couldn't argue with that. If Terrance found ten dollars on the street he'd take out a newspaper advertisement to find the owner.

"And besides it's not that we didn't really like each other," Ethan continued, "The real battle was over what it always is for men – a woman."

I was curious now. "What woman?"

Ethan smiled like a Cheshire cat. "You of course."

"Me?" I laughed out loud. "Sure it was? You're what

seven years younger than us. When we were seniors you were in the sixth grade."

"Seventh grade. Old enough to recognize a hot chick."

Amused, I shook my head. "You're so silly."

"And I wasn't in seventh grade five years ago when you were taking care of your dad," he said, his voice becoming less playful. "The season was over. I was in town then."

"I remember," I confessed, pausing reflectively. I also remembered his attending the wake and funeral, the amazing flowers he sent to the house and the huge donation he made in my father's name to the cancer center. "You were extremely generous."

Ethan smiled reminiscently. "That was just money." He tilted his glass back and forth and I thought he had the strongest looking hands I'd ever seen. He cleared his throat and pulled me from the thoughts I was having about those hands. "I wanted to make you smile, but you'd been home for over a month and every time I saw you all I saw was your pain," he paused as if reflecting. "Smiling after the death of a parent is a tall order, but it broke my heart to see you so heartbroken." He took my hand in his and leaned closer. "I never had a chance to tell you this, but I really appreciated the fact that you attended my games."

My breath caught in my throat. I had no idea what he was wearing, but his cologne had been made for him, because the aroma coming from his pores was sensually perfect. He was making me nervous. I slid my hand from under his warm touch. "Everyone in Garrison was at your games." I recalled how sick I'd been on the way home, so I hadn't been back with the crowd that gathered once a month to travel by bus across the state of Georgia to Southern University for Ethan's soccer game. "I only made it to one."

His lips curved into a lazy smile. "True, but I remember you being at both my games at Monmouth University during my senior year. I mean I know you were in New York, but Central Jersey was a good haul for you. That was special." He nodded like the memory made him proud. "I told my teammates you were my future wife."

"What?" Attempting to hide the fact that I was blushing, I raised my glass to my lips and held it there. "Why would you've said that?"

"Because you looked good in those stands." He laughed. "My teammates would ask me, 'What's up with that hot older chick coming to see you?' I admit I stretched the truth a bit."

I slapped his arm. "No you didn't. What did you say?"

He smiled wide and attractive lines fanned out around his eyes. "Nothing too bad. Just that I'd had a crush on you in high school and now you were interested in me."

"You know you should be ashamed to admit this, don't you?" I felt heat rise to my face. Embarrassed, I covered it. "You men talk worse than women."

Ethan pulled my hand away from my face. His expression became serious. "That was a little more than talk. It was wishful thinking."

The waitress interrupted and placed a glass of iced tea in front of him. She also refilled my glass, smiled at him again and moved to a neighboring table.

"Anyway, you were in New York. I graduated and was off to Europe." The look on his face revealed that had been a happy time for him. "I was hoping you'd come to my going away party, so I could tell you how much it meant for you to be in Jersey, but you were a no show." He tapped his long fingers on the table a few times. They caught my eye. He had nice hands. I remembered how he'd stroked the piano last night. I raised my eyes to his and sensed my not attending his party had been a disappointment to him.

I cleared my throat of the guilt I was suddenly feeling. "I had a big wedding that weekend. I wanted to celebrate with everyone. Garrison was so proud of you. I was proud, but that wedding put my business on the map. It had been planned way too far in advance for me to hand it off."

He frowned. "No sweat. I was mature enough to understand that," he said. "Plus, I knew Terrance was still sprung on you." He chuckled. "Then when your dad got sick, my cousin worked his way back into your life." He raised his glass and took a long sip. "And for what?" He shook his head. "So, he could tell you he was too country to ever leave Coweta County?"

In an effort to keep the pain of that to myself, I lowered my eyes to my iPad again. "That was between us."

"I suppose it was, but I lost respect for him then. Here he had a chance to be with an amazing woman and he was going to throw it all away to stay up under his mama's skirt."

I returned my eyes to his. "He had a good job."

"It was weak. He could have given you guys a chance. The plant wasn't going anywhere. His father could always get him on there if he came back to Garrison. Besides, if he hadn't been in the way I would have made my move."

I sat back and crossed my hands over my chest. "That would have been a waste, because I have rule about dating younger men."

"Yeah, what is it?"

I shrugged. "I don't do it."

Ethan raised his hand to his heart. "I'm so disappointed. What kind of a rule is that?"

A humming sound came from inside his pocket.

Glad for the interruption, I waited for him to answer his phone, but he didn't seem to have any plans to. I asked,

"Aren't you going to get that? It might be your girlfriend."

"I don't have a girlfriend, but I do have voicemail, so tell me why you don't date younger men."

Suddenly feeling a little silly about my answer, I shied away from his gaze. "I never want to be called a cougar and I don't ever want the man in my life looking younger than me."

Ethan chuckled and threw his head back. "Stop the madness woman. Black don't crack, and for the record, you don't look a single hour over twenty-eight."

I worked hard to be as diva divine as I was, so I was flattered, but I wasn't going to let it show. I shook my head. "I live in New York. You live wherever you land, so we don't need to have this 'not happening dot com' discussion." I stood, looked at my watch and said, "I need to meet with the florist."

He stood with me. "We'll continue this conversation at dinner."

I reached for my check. "If you plan to talk about this at dinner then let's go ahead and cancel."

He took my hand and pulled the slip from it. "I've got this." He let his eyes sweep my body. "I promise. No more stories about how I've been in love with you since I was ten."

My heart was racing. This was the first time in years I felt like I had weights in my heels. I couldn't move. He'd actually paralyzed me with those eyes. I cleared my throat and pulled myself together. "I'll be ready at six," I replied, forcing myself to move. That was some serious flirting. I left the restaurant with a ding in the air above me and a little more pep in my step.

Chapter 5

I was ridiculously excited about seeing Ethan again. It was only five thirty and I was showered, dressed and putting on makeup. Technically it wasn't a date. We were hanging out, keeping each other from being bored to death in Garrison, and taking my mind off the only wedding that I've ever not wanted to plan.

As if she could tell I was thinking about her, Janette entered the room and plopped down on my bed. She looked tired and her feet seemed to be a bit swollen. She stood all day at the salon, but she'd been home for hours and they'd been up the entire time.

"Where are y'all going to eat?" she asked.

"A new place in town. Palermo's," I replied, thinking I'd kill two birds with one stone and check the place out as a potential spot for her bridal shower party.

"I heard that was nice. Terrance and I were planning to go, but he's been so busy working lately that he's hardly had time for dinners out like that."

"Really? Is the plant that busy?" I asked, misting my hair with a moisturizer.

"Not at the plant. He's trying to get some business off the ground and he hasn't shared the details with me yet. That's why our money has been kinda short too."

I raised an eyebrow. I couldn't imagine marrying someone who was starting a business that I didn't have the details about, but I wasn't my sister. She would go with the flow assuming Terrance wouldn't have them in the poor house.

"I appreciate you pitching in and paying for stuff for the

wedding. Don't think I don't know it's costing you a lot. I promise if things take off with Terrance's plans, I'll pay you back with interest."

I didn't respond to that. We both knew that money she'd borrowed had never been repaid, no matter how big or small. I met her eyes making sure mine held a smile. Janette seemed so tiny and fragile, much tinier than she ever had when we were growing up. Maybe I had been wrong to go to New York after college. I'd left her all alone and now here she was pregnant before marriage. That wasn't what our father would have wanted for her. I was certain it wasn't what she wanted for herself. I had promised to take care of her, but instead I had abandoned her to go live my dreams. I hadn't even invited her to come live with me once I'd gotten established. I rationalized that she was safer in a small town like Garrison, surrounded by people she knew than in the big city of New York with oftentimes unfriendly strangers.

She stretched out on my bed. "You know you need to watch Ethan. He can be a bit of a canine when it comes to the ladies."

"Really." I tried to keep my interest out of my voice. "I didn't know he had that reputation."

"How would you? You don't live here anymore." She reached for a novel I had been reading, looked at the back cover and continued her warning about him. "Anyway, he didn't have that reputation before he went all over the place and became worldly. He's been overseas with Spanish and Italian women. I follow all the blogs."

"French and Spanish."

"What?" Janette asked.

"He played in France and Spain, so it was French and Spanish women."

Janette shrugged as she should have. I had a horrible

habit of correcting her on facts, not because I wanted to be right, but because I wanted her to be right. I reasoned it was a big sister thing.

"Spanish, French. It's all the same," she said. "I'm surprised he still dates black women."

"He was dating that supermodel. What was her name?"

"Concei?" Janette sucked her teeth. "She doesn't count. She's from Kenya."

I raised an eyebrow. "Kenyans aren't black?"

"You now what I mean. She's worldly like him."

I shrugged, applied lip gloss and lie down across the bed opposite my sister. I wasn't quite sure what she meant by worldly. Worldly as in not a resident of Garrison or worldly as in spiritually, but because I was feigning indifference I didn't bother to ask. "It doesn't matter what kind of women he likes. It's not a date. We're just old friends having dinner."

"Good," Janette replied nonchalantly. "Supermodel competition could make you crazy and besides you're too old for him anyway. He's younger than me."

I nodded. "I'm aware of that."

"You don't want to get a bad reputation in your hometown for being a cheetah that's running around with a younger man."

I rolled my eyes. "It's cougar."

"Huh?" Although Janette should have been able to figure that one out, she looked confused.

"It's cougar when you date a younger man, not cheetah."

She shrugged. "Some kind of fast tail cat."

"Cougars prey on younger men. It doesn't really apply if you're just dating or in an actual relationship."

Janette rolled her neck and grunted. "I know you not laying here trying to justify dating Ethan."

I didn't think my sister who was marrying my ex had the right to impose restrictions on me. "I'm not dating Ethan." My tone was sharper than I'd intended it to be. I took the temper out of my voice. "I'm just clarifying what a cougar actually is."

Janette dropped her head on a pillow and closed her eyes. "Well he don't stay put for long no way, so he's not hardly worth having folks whispering about you."

I wondered if my sister had considered that the only reputation she should be concerned about at this point was hers. She was the one who was unmarried and six months pregnant, not to mention planning to parade herself down the aisle in white. If folks were going to be whispering it wasn't going to be about Ethan and me.

"I guess I could be wrong about him. He might be trying to settle down," she said. "He's been here a long time. He's never hung around Garrison this long. Maybe he's seeing somebody that we don't know about." She was thoughtful. "Maybe someone in Atlanta. I bet it's a celebrity. There are lots of reality T.V. stars in Atlanta."

We were silent for a moment. I, knowing why he was here, and she clearly not.

"Even if he is trying to settle down, I know you aren't trying to date nobody who ain't saved," she added. "Daddy would roll over in his grave."

Now she had my attention. Ethan had grown up in the church. I'd seen him get baptized and take communion like the rest of us. "What makes you say Ethan isn't saved?"

Janette opened her eyes and turned her head towards me. "He's not. He hasn't been in a church since high school."

"How would you know that?"

"His uncle is a preacher. Whenever he comes home he doesn't go to Mount Moriah. It's pretty obvious. Besides, Terrance told me he wasn't. Something about his mama dying when he was young." Janette grunted. "It always amazes me how some people use stuff like that as an excuse. I don't even remember my mama, but I'm not blaming God for it." She sat up and fluffed out her hair.

I was thoughtful about that point. "I guess people handle things differently."

Janette shrugged. "That's why he pimped out that house. Nobody can stay in Pastor Wright's house without going to church."

Now she was getting on my nerves. Everything she was saying was an assumption, just a bunch of gossip and speculation. "He's twenty-nine, Janette. He should have a house of his own. Besides do you know how much money Ethan made playing soccer and doing endorsements? He needs all the tax write offs he can get."

"Stand up for him all you want Miss Cougar, but don't fall for him. He'll break your heart and fly away."

It was on the tip of my tongue to say the last man who broke my heart was hers. The fact that he wouldn't fly out of Garrison had been the end of us, but of course I didn't. I merely shook my head.

Janette stood and stretched like a bored cat. "I need to go on to the church, but when I get home I'm going right to bed."

I took a good look at her. "Maybe you should do that now. You look worn out."

"I don't miss Bible study, especially now that this red scarlet letter is branded on my forehead."

We giggled. "Honey, it's going to be alright in about nine days."

"It will won't it?" She was thoughtful. "Nine more days and I'll be Mrs. Terrance Wright."

She walked out of the room. I felt a stabbing pain in my heart. I'd dubbed myself Mrs. Terrance Wright in high school and now my sister would have the title. I sighed. This was too weird.

I lie on the bed for a few minutes listening to my sister move around downstairs, then outside and eventually heard her car start and pull away. I had yet to ask her where she and Mr. Terrance Wright were planning to live. This house was bigger than the one Terrance owned or rented or whatever was his situation. I'd been afraid to ask her, not wanting to learn that that they would reside here and raise their babies in this house, because if they did it would no longer feel like home.

I rolled over on my stomach and pressed my made-up face into the comforter. I just didn't know. Everything about her choice of husband made the marriage difficult for me to stomach. Of course she hadn't been thinking about that when she'd gone out and slept with him. I groaned. Now I knew for sure why you stayed away from the exes. I'd never really thought about the implications of it before. I just knew to follow the rule. Whomever had made it had to be a woman that had been through this "ish", because only someone who had been where I was could possibly understand all the factors that could come into play when someone close to you dated an ex.

I stood and surveyed myself one more time in the mirror. The makeup made me look like I was going on a date. I couldn't have Ethan thinking I was going to break my "no dating younger men" rule. There was enough rule breaking going on right now. Besides, he was Terrance's cousin, dating me would mean he was with Terrance's ex.

Did men care about that? I wasn't sure.

"Why are you even going there in your mind?" I asked my reflection. "Ethan is a friend and he wouldn't ever be anything more." I walked into the bathroom that joined my bedroom to my sisters and washed the makeup off my face, reapplied my moisturizer and a little lip gloss just as the doorbell rang. I turned to leave the room and then turned back to the mirror and pointed at myself. "Ethan is just a friend," I repeated. "He's twenty-nine, Terrance's cousin, and he appears to be backslidden. They'll be no opening your mouth tonight."

I flipped the light switch to the off position and made my way down the stairs. I pulled the door open and all that I'd just told myself seemed to evaporate into a mist in the sky. Ethan was standing there looking all kinds of yummy and chocolaty. Once that woodsy scent coming off his body hit my nostrils all I could think was that I wanted to break every rule I had ever made.

***

Palermo's was upscale for Garrison. Crisp white tablecloths, wait staff in white and black moving about with their hands behind their backs and what appeared to be fine china on the tables. I thought about Renea's desire to hold the bridal shower here all on my tab and knew that chick had to be crazy. If everybody came that showed up at the house last night this was going to be a thousand dollar party and that's if they didn't order a bunch of liquor.

Ethan didn't seem at all phased by the fanciness. I was sure he'd grown accustomed to eating in places much more posh when he was dining overseas. He'd been curiously quiet in the car and I started to feel insecure like he'd wished he'd known about my dating rules prior to making the commitment. He wasn't alone in these thoughts. I wish I hadn't let him put his tongue in my mouth prior to knowing he was no longer in love with Jesus. Not loving the Lord was for sure a deal breaker. Relationships were hard when you were spiritually incompatible, but he sure smelled good.

"Mr. Wright!" The maître d exclaimed. "It's a pleasure to have you with us at Palermo's this evening. Madame." He took my hand and gave it a little shake. "Please come this way."

The restaurant was designed in a circle with a sunken center that included tables on both levels. We were seated in a less than private location on the second floor. He put menus in front of us and pulled out my chair. "Sir, the owners would like it if you accepted dinner on the house. We appreciate you joining us."

Ethan said a simple thank you and the maître d disappeared.

I raised an eyebrow. "Wow, no wonder you have so much money. Do you get to eat free all over the world?"

"When people recognize me," he replied. "I prefer to pay and keep my privacy. You see where he put us. I'll be in the local paper tomorrow and before this meal is over we'll be interrupted for several autograph and picture taking sessions."

"Doesn't sound like a bad problem to have," I said.

"It's not, unless it's your problem." He sighed. "I'm not complaining. I loved playing soccer and I like being rich."

I smiled and then so did he for the first time since he'd stood in my door.

I opened my menu. "I'm glad to finally see a smile."

"I apologize if I'm not good company. I found out one of my former teammates was killed in a boating accident this morning. I'm kind of in shock."

I felt horrible. How selfish I had been for wanting the chipper Ethan who'd taken my mind off my problems. I reached across the table for his hand and squeezed it. "I'm so sorry to hear that. Please forgive me for not sensing something deeper was wrong."

Ethan squeezed my hand back. "It's okay. How could you? We hardly know each other." He opened his menu and mumbled. "Not that I don't want that to change."

I smiled inwardly. It was nice to have the complimentary Ethan back. I had to admit the attention he showered on me made me feel special.

A waiter interrupted us to take our drink and menu selections. Once he was gone we resumed our conversation.

"So, do you want to talk about your friend?" I took a sip of water and helped the still somber Ethan with a prompt. "How old was he? Which team did he play for La Rojas or Tricolores?"

"You know the teams I played for?" he chuckled. "Someone has been using Google."

I brushed my hair off my shoulders and raised my neck proudly. "What makes you think I had to Google you? Would it surprise you to know that I followed your career?"

Ethan's face took on a serious look. "Yes it would. I'd be surprised to know you cared."

"You're our local celebrity." I nodded past him. "And that's about to be confirmed right now."

A man and a boy who looked about ten years old approached our table with a notebook in hand.

"Mr. Wright, I don't mean to disturb your dinner, but my son and I are big fans. If you and the lady," he glanced toward me, "don't mind the interruption, my son would love a picture and your autograph."

Ethan lifted the child onto his lap. "Of course." He looked at me and made the biggest smile he could manage. "Do I have anything in my teeth?

I giggled and shook my head. "You look fine."

He turned the boy toward him. "What about you, dude? Do you have anything in your teeth?" The child laughed and opened wide so Ethan could inspect his mouth. "Nah, you're good. They both turned to face his father and after a few flashes of light and Ethan's signature on the pad, they were gone.

I sat back and crossed my arms. "I'm impressed."

"Don't be. Making kids laugh and playing soccer come natural to me. Be more impressed that I learned to play that piano."

The waiter returned with our drinks and bread. I reached for my water goblet. "Speaking of which, I didn't get to ask you how you learned to play."

He snapped a finger and wagged it. "Yeah, that's because I was too busy trying to get that long overdue kiss out of you."

I pinned him with a look. The old Ethan had definitely resurfaced.

He tossed his head back a bit. "I'm just saying, I remember how it went down last night." He smiled. "I took lessons when I was in France. It was kind of lonely and boring being in a foreign country. Taking lessons assured me that I would have something to do on Tuesday and Thursday afternoons. Plus the teacher spoke English, fluently and that was what I was looking for. Most of my teammates spoke French. The coach spoke French. I didn't have anybody to talk to. I tried to learn the language, but you know you're never fluent so…"

I nodded. "Impressive."

"Yes, be impressed with that. Learning piano was hard."

"You make it look easy."

"Well, I had my heart in it last night." His gaze was more than smoldering under the dim restaurant lights. We chatted a little more about his piano lessons and then we were served our salads and more bread.

I bowed my head for grace and noticed that Ethan did as well, but he certainly hadn't taken the lead on it. The sadness he'd exuded earlier crept back over him.

"We hadn't finished talking about your friend," I said.

"You could tell I was thinking about him. I'm sorry to be bad company for you."

"You're not." I shook my head. "I want to know about him, so please tell me."

"We played together in France. He was from South Africa, the oldest of fourteen children. He loved the game, but loved that he was in a position to take care of his family at home even more."

"That's a wonderful testament to his life that he cared for his family."

"Yeah, but such a waste. He was still playing."

"Tragedies like that are so hard, but I suppose there's a reason for everything." I put an elbow on the table and rested my chin on my fist. "What do you think about that?"

Ethan's eyes had been lowered. He raised them and I could see the pain. "I don't know. I guess it'll all make sense one day." He took a long sip of his water. "Traveling the world and seeing some of the suffering makes it difficult to understand, so I admit to having a great many doubts over the years."

My cell phone rang one of my special ringtones. I reached into my purse for it. "This is Janette. Let me see what she wants." I pushed the talk button expecting to hear my sister's voice. "Terrance.... yes." I listened to him and ended the call just as the waiter arrived with our plates. "We need to take this to go," I said and then I turned to Ethan. "Would you mind taking me to the hospital? Janette's in labor."

Chapter 6

Ethan and I rushed to *Garrison General Hospital* and made it into the emergency room before the rims stopped spinning on his monster truck. We reached Janette's room and upon entering things appeared deceptively calm. Janette was hooked up to a monitor that reported the baby's heartbeat and revealed if she was having any contractions. She wasn't hanging upside down and I guessed she hadn't had her cervix sewn up or any of the other horrible things I heard they did to women to keep babies from sliding out.

Terrance stood from a chair in the corner that looked way too tiny for a man of his height. "Thank you for coming," he said to me and then he looked at his cousin and simply nodded. "I forgot you didn't have a car. Ethan, I appreciate you bringing her."

"No problem. We were together," Ethan said. Not together at dinner. Just together. Although he should have remembered we were having dinner, for some reason Terrance didn't look particularly happy to hear that.

More pissing in the pond, I thought. *Men.*

I interrupted. "What's going on with Janette? How could she be in labor so early?"

"I'm right here," Janette's voice was weak. "You don't have to talk like I'm not."

I joined Janette at her bedside. She reached for my hand. "They gave me medicine to stop the contractions from coming. I was having preterm labor." She played around with the pillows behind her and then she seemed to remember she was in a hospital bed and used the button to raise the head of the bed.

"Preterm labor. How far along are you?" I asked.

"I'm twenty-eight weeks."

"Much too early to have the baby." Terrance took her hand on the other side of the bed. "The doctor says she's dehydrated, so they're giving her some fluids and she's going to be on bed rest for a few weeks."

"Bed rest," Ethan interjected. "Does that mean you have to stay in the hospital?"

"Heavens no. I'm probably going to be released tonight, but I have to take it easy. Keep my feet up and get plenty of rest."

"And she has to drink lots of water." Terrance added.

Janette grimaced. "My favorite thing."

"But there's no reason to think the baby won't go full term?" My statement was more of a question.

"No reason at all," Terrance replied. "She just has to follow doctor's orders.

We all stood around for another five minutes or so just looking at Janette breathe and listening to the monitor beep. A nurse came in, looked at the tape from the monitor and took Janette's vitals including her blood pressure and heartbeat.

"Visiting hours end at eight." She raised five fingers on one hand and three on the other as she exited the room.

I looked at Ethan and he laughed. "She probably missed her true calling. She should have been a kindergarten teacher."

I couldn't help but chuckle and so did Janette.

"Ethan Wright, don't you make me laugh this baby out of my belly," Janette said firmly. "Oh God, I think I need to pee."

"I'll help you," I shoved my purse in Ethan's hands. "You can hold that since you made her have to go."

Terrance and I helped Janette down from the bed, unstrapped her monitor and I walked her into the ladies room. Upon her arrival there she realized she didn't have to go after all, so we made the way back to the bed. The men stepped out of the room while I helped her back into bed.

"You and Ethan look friendly," she said.

"That's because we're friends."

"He's not looking at you like he's thinking about friendship." Janette wagged a finger. "Be careful with him or you'll end up like me without the ring."

"Stay in your lane, little sister." I reconnected her monitor. Then before she could utter another warning I yelled toward the door. "Guys you can come in!"

After another five minutes of very few words, I finally asked the question that had been floating around in my mind since I'd entered the room. "The wedding? Will you still be having it?"

Terrance answered for Janette. "No reason we can't still have it, but the running around…well let's just say we're glad you're here, Nec –," he raised his hand to cover a fake cough. "—Deniece."

Terrance's eyes met mine for a moment. For the first time in our adult lives, I couldn't get a read on him. Every time we were in the same room I felt his presence pressing me for something, but I had no idea what it was. It was an energy that I couldn't put my finger on, but for the most part it felt negative or at least that was how I was channeling it.

Ethan cleared his throat. "I'm double parked. I'm going to go move the truck before it gets towed." He handed me my bag. "I can wait for you out there."

I stopped him with a hand on his arm. I didn't want to be alone with the two of them. Janette I didn't mind. She was my sister. She'd always been my sister and as much as she sometimes worked my nerves, that was nothing new, but this feeling of uneasiness that I had around Terrance was and I wasn't going to subject myself to it. "Janette is there anything we can do? It's seven forty-five. They'll ask us to leave soon."

"Could you make sure there's some Butter Pecan in the house from Dolans? I'll be wanting some when I get home."

I looked at Ethan and we both looked back to Janette and nodded. "Is that it, honey?"

Janette was thoughtful for a moment. "I think that's it."

I let go of her hand and gave her thigh a little squeeze. "Okay, then we're going to go. I'll be at the house when you get there."

"Okay," Janette said. "Thanks for coming Ethan." She turned over to her side and closed her eyes.

"We'll get that ice cream," Ethan offered. Then he extended a hand. "Terrance."

Terrance hesitated, but then swallowed and shook. I thought it odd for him to hesitate when they were in business together to the tune of nearly a million dollars, but some things never changed. Terrance had always been jealous of Ethan. At first it was because of the attention Mother Wright doted on the poor motherless child, then later for his stardom and now I suppose it was the money that came with the stardom.

We turned to walk out of the room and Janette said, "Wait. Before you leave, we should have prayer."

Terrance cracked a tentative smile.

"Of course." I reentered the room.

Ethan did not join me. He merely nodded and said, "I'll meet you at the truck."

***

Ethan and I stopped at Dolan's Ice Cream shop and made it in right before the owner, Joe Dolan closed for the evening. Garrison was a quiet town and businesses didn't stay open very late. Dolan's turned the closed sign around at eight-thirty during the week giving folks who had after dinner cravings an opportunity to finish the dishes and still make it there in time.

We purchased a quart of Butter Pecan for Janette and our favorites for ourselves. We arrived at the house and sat in the truck for a few minutes. It was dark and looked lonely. It was funny, I lived alone, but there was something about being in Garrison right now that made me feel lonely in my aloneness, so I invited Ethan in. "No point in us eating alone," I said, offering an explanation for the invitation. "I can warm up our food and you can keep me company for a little while longer if like."

"I can't think of anything else I'd prefer to do." Ethan turned off the ignition, came around the truck, opened the door for me and reached in for our bags.

We entered the dark house. I flooded the living room and dining room with light in an effort to not create atmosphere. Then I washed my hands and began to microwave our food.

"You can turn on the television," I yelled to him from the kitchen.

"Not much of a T.V person," he responded. "I'll wash up and set the table." He did just that. When I crossed into the dining room from the kitchen I noticed the recessed lighting had been dimmed a bit and there was soft jazz music streaming from his cell phone. He took the plates from my hand and put them down on place mats that he'd positioned next to each other on the table.

"This is cozy," I said, taking the chair he'd pulled out for me.

"I'm trying to recapture the atmosphere in Palermo's."

"Minus the autograph seekers," I chuckled.

"I can sign something for you."

I raised an eyebrow. "I've known you too long to be an autograph hound."

"You never know," he said. "Maybe one day you'll want my name on something."

I laughed. "I am not going to ask you to explain that one."

He laughed too. "I was envisioning a tattoo right there in the center of your chest."

"I can guarantee you that you'll never see your name in the center of my chest, Mr. Wright."

"Well, maybe I'll just sign it on your heart."

I laughed. "Now you're trying too hard."

Ethan chuckled. "I thought that was original."

Our eyes caught for a long, intense moment. I fought the desire to look away, but in the end his resolve was stronger, because I dropped my eyes.

I reached for my glass and cleared my throat. "Why are you staring?"

Ethan reached for his glass and took a long sip before answering. "I can't help myself. You're beautiful."

I know I turned fifty shades of blush. "Thank you.

That's nice to hear."

He was quick with his response. "It's easy to say." Still, his soul searching eyes remained on me.

I cleared my throat. "Our food is cooling again."

"Then let's eat." Ethan picked up his fork, gave me a teasing smile and delved into his plate.

I was finally able to breathe.

We ate in silence for a few minutes. The music and Ethan's occasional glances in my direction served to turn up the heat in the room a bit more than the hot peppers in my entrée.

I put my fork down. "I can't eat another bite. It's nearly nine." I stood from the table. "I'm going to check on Janette."

Ethan pushed back from the table as well, but his plate was empty. He'd inhaled his food whole.

I reached into my bag and pushed the numbers for Garrison General. I was surprised I still remembered it, but I guess it was permanently etched on my brain from all the calls I placed when my dad was sick.

After a few rings, I heard Terrance's voice on the other end. I passed on greeting him. "How's Janette?"

"She's fine. Sleeping. She's had a few more contractions, so they still have her under observation. I'm not sure she'll be home tonight," he said and paused, "I'm not sure I want her to be. It feels safer here."

"Okay, let her know I'm thinking about her. Praying for her," I replied.

"I will."

"Call my cell if things change. I'm going to lock up after Ethan leaves and –"

He interrupted me before I could finish my sentence. "Ethan is still there?"

I turned my back to Ethan a bit and whispered. "That's none of your business."

"I'm concerned is all. I know my cousin can be an interesting kind of guy."

"Well, I like interesting. It's better than boring," I snapped nastily.

"Are you implying that I'm boring because I didn't want to move to New York?"

"I'm not implying –" I stopped myself. What was I doing? I didn't argue with Terrance when we were dating. I certainly wasn't going to argue with him now that we weren't. "Give Janette my love." I pushed the end button and twisted back around in my seat to face Ethan again.

"Janette's fine, but I gather Terrance is not."

I shook my head. "I don't know what's going on with him."

"He's nervous about the marriage, feeling guilty about the pregnancy and you and also hating the fact that you're with me. It's enough to make a preacher's boy reach for the bottle."

I shook my head. "That's ridiculous."

"He's eating his cake and wanting it too."

"Men."

"Can't live with them. Can't live with them." Ethan winked.

I laughed at the play on words. "Just can't live with them," I said. "Do you want your ice cream?"

He stretched like a cat and rubbed his belly. "I've got some more room, but can we take it in the living room?"

"I'll meet you there."

The television was on when I entered the living room with our bowls of ice cream. "I thought I was going to have to watch the football game."

"I won't bore you," he said taking his bowl. "My favorite crime drama is on BBC America."

I sat down and folded my legs under my bottom. I could still do that thanks to yoga. "I can't say I watch British television."

"You'll love this. It's a psychological thriller. Cop show."

Ethan sounded excited. I was not. "I scare easy."

"I'll protect you." He flashed that million dollar smile that I'd seen on countless magazine covers, blogs and television clips. He was much more handsome in person. I'd never really noticed. I guess Terrance was throwing shade.

"You won't be here all night."

"I can sleep on this sofa. I'm very disciplined. It's yourself you'll have to worry about." He winked and shoved a large spoon of ice cream in his mouth. I pursed my lips. Ethan laughed. "I'm messing with you. It's so much fun. I can't remember the last time I've been with a grown woman that blushed so much."

"Blush?" I avoided his eyes by digging around in my ice cream bowl. "I'm not blushing."

"You've been blushing all day. It started in the tuxedo shop." He put more ice cream in his mouth. "Don't worry. It's a good thing. A sign of innocence and that's rare."

"Are you sure it's innocence and not naïvety?"

Ethan squinted. "You would never have survived in New York City for this long if you were naïve."

"It's possible to be savvy in business and not so smart in

your personal life."

"That's true, but are you questioning yourself because of Terrance or does some other fool have you twisted?" he asked.

I sighed and put my bowl down. "I'm not questioning myself at all or at least I didn't think I was."

"Well, I know one thing you need to question and that's making rules about who to date and who not to date, especially that age thing."

I pulled back my neck and looked him up and down. "Would that be because that age thing pertains to you?"

"Nah," he shook his head. "I'm not the least bit interested in you."

He laughed out loud and I joined him. I wasn't sure if I was supposed to be. Had I misread him?

"Seriously," he continued. "You could miss out on a really nice guy by setting that kind of limitation and you could end up with a real jerk that's just the right age for you."

"Ethan…"

He raised a hand to shush me. "I said my piece." He picked up the remote and unmuted the volume. "Let's watch the Brits."

Chapter 7

I woke to the sound of my cell phone ringing, the smell of Ethan's woodsy cologne and the feel of his hand on my knee. I careened my neck in the direction of the ring and in the sliver of moonlight noted the time on the face of the clock. It was just after four a.m. I gasped. Ethan stirred, but didn't wake. I tried to remember how I ended up on a couch in my father's house with a twenty-nine year old, hot millionaire and then I remembered, Janette, the wedding…preterm labor, hence the four a.m. phone call. It had to be Terrance.

I moved Ethan's hand and he bolted upright like my knee had been the pillow his head rested on. I stood, stretched and moved in the dimmed light for my purse.

"I was having a very good dream." I heard Ethan groan behind me.

When I reached the door I could see headlights bouncing against the house and recognized Terrance's truck. I reached into my bag for my cell, removed it and returned his call.

"What's going on? Is Janette okay?"

"She's fine." His tone was terse. "She's with me."

I pulled the phone away from my ear and looked at it like I hadn't heard what I thought I heard. "Why are you sitting in the truck?"

Ethan came up behind me and asked, "Is everything okay?"

I moved the phone from my ear and pointed out the door.

Ethan squinted. "Is that Terrance?"

I nodded and returned the phone to my ear.

"I didn't want to walk in on anything," Terrance replied.

"Don't worry about it. We're almost dressed so you can come on in." I pressed the button to end the call.

Ethan was noticeably shocked. "Wow! You are mad at him."

"What do you mean? I'm not…" I paused mid sentence. "I'm not mad. I'm just, I don't know."

"That was beyond angry," Ethan said. "Pretending you and I –" I shot him a sharp look. He shook his head. "What a waste of my rep. I didn't even do anything but watch bad television."

The headlights on the truck dimmed. I moved to the table and picked up our ice cream bowls and glasses and took them into the kitchen. Why had I done that? Why do I want to make Terrance angry? And more importantly, why does he care?

I heard the screen door snap and readied myself to return to the living room.

Janette had just taken a seat in her favorite chair when I entered. Terrance stood next to her, hand on her shoulder and his face twisted as if he'd just eaten some sour grapes. "You two seem cozy," she said.

Ethan and I looked at each other. He smiled a little. I cleared my throat. "I didn't know they discharged patients this time of morning."

"They send pregnant women home as soon as they finish monitoring them," Terrance replied. "Plus, your sister insisted she wanted to come home and finish the night in her bed and wake up to her bathroom."

"How are you feeling?" Ethan asked.

"Better. I think the fluids from the I.V. helped hydrate me. I'll be good as new in a few days."

"Great." Ethan nodded.

A beat of silence passed between the four of us.

"You ladies could use some sleep and so could I," Ethan said. "I should be going."

"I'm sure you should," Terrance replied, through gritted teeth.

Ethan had been walking toward the door, but Terrance's comment stopped him dead in his tracks. "What's your problem? You've been trippin' for days?"

"I don't have a problem. I'm just disgusted that you've forgotten what a small town Garrison is."

"Meaning?"

"Meaning you've got no business leaving this house this early in the morning."

Ethan rubbed a hand over his bald head and shook it. "Have you lost your mind?" he asked through gritted teeth. "I'm grown. You're not talking to the boys in your youth group."

Terrance removed his hand from Janette's shoulder and made a bee line right to Ethan with a pointed finger. "Then act like it. Grown people take responsibility. You should care about Deniece's reputation."

Ethan waved his hand in front of him, knocking Terrance's finger out of his face. "Reputation? If people are talking, it's about their preacher's son knocking up his ex-girlfriend's sister."

Terrance looked hurt at first, but then without warning he hauled off and punched Ethan in the face. Ethan hit the ground, stayed there for a few seconds like he was trying to decide what he was going to do. Decision made, he sprang up and charged Terrance. The two flew out of the door, onto the porch and down on the grass with a loud thud. I couldn't believe it. Janette screamed and I ran out the door behind them.

"Stop!" I yelled, pulling on Ethan's arm.

I heard Janette on the porch screaming for Ethan to get off Terrance. After few moments of my pleading and a few good body shots, Ethan stopped. He wrenched Terrance's badly torn shirt again for good measure and stood to his feet. "Try me again."

"Are you two crazy?" I put my body between them, just in case one of them decided they weren't done hitting the other.

Ethan stormed off in the direction of his truck.

I followed. "Are you okay?"

He turned and looked at me like I had to be joking. "That was nothing. Terrance and I have been fighting since we were kids."

He had a cut over his eye, probably a slit opened by Terrance's class ring. "I've never heard of you getting into a fight on the field." I leaned close to his face and raised a hand to his eye to examine the damage. "I don't think you need stitches, but let me get something for it."

He dabbed at it with the tail of his shirt. "It's fine. I'll take care of it when I get home."

I put a hand on his arm. "At least let me get a tissue and some ice to stop the bleeding."

"I've gotten much worse playing soccer, babe." He smiled and I realized he probably had. "Have lunch with me tomorrow?"

He caught me off guard. An invitation was the last thing I was expecting while he was recovering from a fist fight. I sighed and shook my head. "I need to keep an eye on Janette."

"Dinner," he insisted. "Terrance can take care of his woman when he gets off work."

He was probably right about that and as it had been, I had no interest being in the house with the lovers, but I was noncommittal. "Call me."

"Answer your phone or I'll show up." He kissed my cheek like we were lovers, climbed into his truck and drove away.

The kiss. Such a simple gesture, but it felt right like he had been doing it forever. I shook it off and turned around to find Janette attempting to nurse her man's wounds. Terrance was sitting on the steps dabbing at a bloody lip.

"You should be in the house," he said to Janette.

"I'll get you some ice." I walked past them to go inside.

"Haven't you done enough?" Janette barked.

I stopped in my tracks. "Excuse me. What exactly is that you think I've done?"

"I told you he was trouble. There's no explanation for you to have him here this time of night," Janette said and then corrected herself. "I mean morning."

"I don't need to explain myself. Like Ethan said, we're all adults. This is my house just as much as it is yours. If your man can't be civil and not attack my guest –"

Terrance exploded. "Your guest happens to be my younger cousin. We were raised practically as brothers and I'll say what ever I want to him wherever I want!" He was yelling so loud he had to have ruptured some blood vessels and woke up a neighbor or two.

"Not in this house and not with your fist." I shook my head. "What's happened to you? When did you become such a disrespectful, careless fool?"

Terrance wiped his lip and turned his eyes away from mine.

"That's enough," Janette cried. "Enough for tonight."

"Yes, it is." I snatched the screen door open. "I'm going to bed. You can get your own ice and you can tuck in your fiancé. I'm sure you know where her bedroom is."

I jogged up the stairs to my bedroom and slammed the door against the temper Gayle had warned me would eventually explode.

Chapter 8

Time had never been on my side with respect to this event and now it was even less so. I had eight days to pull all the loose ends together while continuing to run my business in New York. Gayle was great, but only with the vendors and for the administrative details. Brides and their mothers wanted to talk to me, so I spent most of the morning touching base with my clients.

I prepared Janette breakfast and pushed a sixty-four ounce insulated water bottle on her. I also left her with a note pad and pen and assigned her the task of completing her reception playlist for the D.J. Then I settled in the dining room with my iPad, which included a monstrous to-do list and started making phone calls. First up was Renea to let her know that due to Janette's condition, the bridal shower would be held at our house. Renea's dreams of eating at Palermo's would have to be shared with her boyfriend as she would no longer find out how fine or not fine the food was at my expense. In addition to the potluck she offered, I opted to have some of the food catered and placed a call to a family friend who owned a small BBQ restaurant in town. I assigned her to get the Evite out to let all the women know. I'd preferred a hand delivered invitation to each of the guest, but she was clear that "ain't nobody got time for that", and told me her email invitation would suffice.

I moved on to my other calls, which included the photographer, videographer, caterer, soloist, musicians, limo service, manicurist and a follow-up with the florist. I was glad to be able to get most of my work done by telephone because it saved me from having to drive around town all day. Driving was already getting old and I had only been in town a few days. That realization reminded me I needed to stop at the drug store to get some Sea Bands to help with that especially since I was going to have to make a trip to Atlanta to get decorations and wedding favors. There was no way I could drive around the city all day and not be sick.

I pulled up the catalog for a bridal supply store that I'd used in Atlanta for a few local events way back when I was still living in Garrison getting my business started. They were still operating and had vastly updated their offerings, so I was hopeful I could get what I needed as soon as I figured out what that was.

I had no vision for this wedding, which was so unlike me. As soon as I sat down with a client ideas would flow like water down a fall. My choice of career was perfect for me because I could turn any venue into a place fit for royalty to be married, but I was stumped and I knew why. I wanted no part of it from the beginning and I'd yet to put my heart in it. But heart or no heart, I was out of time. I had to execute this, if not for my sister, for my own good. I had my business reputation to protect.

I took a lunch tray to Janette. Like a good girl, she'd compiled a list of music she thought would work for the reception. I took a seat and browsed it. First on the list was "The Closer I Get to You."

I tried to remember the words to the song, something like "Over and over again I tried to tell myself that we could never be more than friends." I rolled my eyes. "Which version of The Closer I Get?"

"What do you mean? Luther and Beyoncé made that."

"Luther and Bey's version is a remake. The original is Roberta Flack and Donnie Hathaway."

Janette frowned. "I don't even know who they are, so go with Luther and Bey."

"Of course." I perused the rest of the list getting more

and more steamed as I thought of the implications of music by Brian McKnight, Kenny Lattimore, and Tony Terry. "Do you think Terrance will be okay with this list or do you need to run it by him?"

Janette pushed her body higher on the pillows. "Terrance doesn't care much. He's not really into secular music, but you already know that."

I eyed my sister suspiciously. Why had she added that tag at the end about my knowing? She had a snitty look on her face, like she wanted to pick a fight. I chalked it up to boredom or discomfort. She didn't want to fight with me. I could leave and let her plan herself right into a wedding day disaster.

"The DJ should have everything," she said. "He did the Dorsey wedding last year and he had every love song ever made."

"Okay, great." iPad in hand, I moved down my list. "We need to talk about your theme. I've been asking you for weeks and now I have to get decorations."

"I don't know, Niecy. Whatever you can make happen with my budget." She picked up the remote control and started flipping though the channels on the muted television.

"Your budget? I'm not sure what that is," I muttered, rolling my eyes.

Janette bit down on her bottom lip. "We only have four thousand dollars left after I take out the money for the video, the photographer and the DJ. That's barely going to cover the rest of the food at the reception so I'm going to have to owe you." She waved a hand. "Do whatever you can."

I looked at the stack of bride magazines on her nightstand. How could she not know what she wanted when she had all those magazines and the Internet? I stood. "I don't want any drama after the wedding if you don't like what I've chosen."

Janette sighed and gave me a polite smile. "I trust you."

I left her room. She trusted me. I had a mind to make it look like a bottle of Pepto Bismol had exploded. Ethan was right, my sister should have eloped.

I entered the dining room to a ringing phone. It was Terŕance. He was last person on the earth I wanted to talk to. I let it go to voicemail. He could check on his fiancé by calling her. I was determined not to have a conversation with him, especially after the way he behaved last night. He may be becoming my brother-in-law, but it didn't mean we had to be friendly. That wasn't ideal. It was never the way I imagined it would be, because family was so important, but I hadn't gotten to that place where I'd forgiven yet. Plus, there was the matter of his jealousy about Ethan. How dare he have an attitude about who I was dating? Did he love my sister or did he just knock her up and now he was going to marry her and make her miserable? I know lots of couples married and grew to love each other, but that wasn't the way it was supposed to be, especially not with a baby in the picture. I resented him for so many things. I just couldn't exchange a word with him without wanting to cuss him out.

I cleared the screen on my phone and noticed I'd missed a call from Ethan. My heart skipped a beat. I plopped down on a chair. What was going on with me? Getting all in like with Terrance's cousin was not in the plan. I lived in New York. He lived wherever he wanted. One Wright man had already been the wrong man for me. Hadn't I had enough? I thought about ignoring his call, but he'd already let me know if I did he'd be showing up here, so I pushed the button and dialed his number.

"I've been thinking about you the entire day. It's taken every ounce of discipline in my body not to have called you already." Ethan said.

I smiled. Talk about a greeting. Who didn't want to hear that?

"I've been talking to vendors all day." I could hear the smile in my own voice.

"So, are you trying to tell me you haven't been thinking about me?" The velvety timbre of his voice dropped an octave and become huskier. I imagined his long body stretched out on a piece of furniture in his family room. That was hot.

"Not really," I teased.

"Not one thought?"

I smiled. I was enjoying this. "You did cross my mind earlier. I wondered how your eye was."

"It's black. It may be black at the wedding."

"Hmmm," I murmured, "there's makeup for that."

"I'm not wearing makeup. It's bad enough I have to put on that suit."

"You've worn makeup every time you've had a photo shoot for a sports magazine. You will not mess up the pictures for a wedding I'm planning. A little makeup won't kill you."

His voice held a chuckle. "You're right, but not seeing you all day will, so what about that dinner?"

I sighed. Gave it some thought. I did need to eat, and I most certainly did not want to be stuck here with Terrance and Janette all evening. "I could stand to get out of the house."

"Great. How about we go into the city and have some real pizza?"

"You forget I live in New York. I have real pizza all the time. As appetizing as that sounds I really don't want to go for that ride. I get car sick pretty easily and I'm going to have to go to Atlanta tomorrow anyway, so I need to save my nausea for then."

Ethan was silent for a moment. "I'm free tomorrow. I could take you."

An image of them shopping for wedding decorations came to her. He'd be bored to death. "I appreciate it, but I couldn't put you out like that."

"Put me out? I said I had nothing to do."

I considered his offer. A truck would be helpful as would someone else behind the wheel other than me. I couldn't deny the idea of spending the day with him was appealing. "Okay, tomorrow is a date, but I don't want any whining about how long it takes me to shop. This wedding stuff can be pretty painful for an onlooker."

"I swear I won't moan or groan," he said.

"I'm going to remind you of that."

"I'll figure out something for dinner. How about I pick you up at five-thirty and surprise you."

I hesitated. "I don't like surprises."

"Of course you don't. Planners never do, but trust me, this'll be cool. Jeans and a tee-shirt okay?"

"Let me confirm the time with Terrance."

"I already did. He said he'd be there at five-thirty and he'll pick something up for Janette."

I remembered the ugly words Terrance and Ethan had exchanged and decided the two men didn't need to see each other this quickly. "In that case pick me up at five-fifteen. I don't want your other eye black."

Ethan laughed. "Trust me. He'll never catch me off guard like that again. I'll see you at quarter after five."

"Okay."

"And Nectar, you can wear jeans, but don't skip the heels."

I laughed. "Say goodbye, Ethan." I pushed the end button.

***

Ethan was right on time and that was good because Terrance was a few minutes early. I spotted his truck turning onto our street. I hustled downstairs and opened the front door so he could let himself in. Then I hid out in the restroom and waited until I heard Ethan's truck. Childish I know, but I had no intentions on letting Terrance get me alone.

While I had no plans to be alone with Terrance, Ethan certainly had plans to be alone with me. His surprise was a dinner made with his own hands served on his deck.

"I tried a few new things," he said. "I catch an occasional cooking show on the television."

I slid into the chair he pulled out for me. "Have you just watched or gotten in some practice?"

"Watched," he replied, opening a fancy jar that looked like fresh steeped ice tea and filling both our glasses.

I raised an eyebrow. "Watching eh, do you think you'd be a great soccer player if you'd just watched the game or even have learned to play the piano without practice?"

He shrugged. "I figured I couldn't mess this up. It's a recipe."

I laughed and reached for my glass. "I'll let you know."

He nodded. "I'm sure you will." He retreated into the

house leaving me to marvel at his deck. I turned and took the entire view in; an outdoor retreat was the accurate description. It was two levels with a massive pergola and an integrated privacy screen at one end. The other end swept down to a hot tub with a pool. The table I was sitting at was a concrete built in. To my right he'd installed an outside kitchen area complete with an enormous stone barbeque grill, which looked like it was turned on. To my left was lounge seating in an outdoor entertainment area that included a television as large as the entire wall space. It had to be sixty inches or more.

I stood and walked to the end of the deck to survey what was on the first level. More seating and a swim-up bar complete with stools at the end of the pool. Amazing.

"I should have told you to bring your suit." Ethan's voice broke my concentration. He opened the lid to the grill and placed the two skewers covered in vegetables on the cooking grate. I joined him just in time to see him flip two humongous steaks.

"How many pounds of meat is that? It literally looks like a side of beef."

"Twenty-four ounce Porterhouses. This is make an impression meat. I reserve it for the very best in dinner guest."

I raised an eyebrow. "It works. I'm impressed. I know you didn't pick these up at Piggly Wiggly."

He shook his head. "I'm a bit of a snob when it comes to my beef. I don't eat much of it, so when I do I prefer grass fed." He closed the grill and put down the fork. "I have a few shipped in when I come home."

I nodded and returned to the edge of the deck. "This is amazing. I'm surprised you built it when you spend so little time here."

One broad shoulder lifted in a shrug. "This is home. I want home to feel like a retreat." He began. "Remember, when I'm building houses and schools and wells we sometimes sleep in some pretty cruddy spots. There aren't any five star hotels in Southern Sudan. Even if there were, we wouldn't stay in them. It's not cool to build houses for the poor and retire to luxurious hotels, so when I'm working I sleep in campsites."

I thought about that, about his sacrifice. How could someone so loving and generous be removed from the God who had gifted him to give? I turned back to him. "I admire you. I haven't slept an uncomfortable night in my life."

He leaned in closer. The effect of the daylight savings had already cast a shadow of darkness that the overhead light worked to compensate for. His eyes were serious. He licked his lips and I was certain he was going to kiss me again. I was going to let him, but then his phone began to beep.

He reached in his pocket. "That's the timer. I have to get the stuff in the kitchen."

I cleared my throat, stepped back a little to get away from his heat. "Let me help."

He shook his head, still never removing his eyes from mine. "No, relax. I like to serve." He made a quick departure back into the house.

He liked to serve. God that had to be a line, because the Lord didn't make them like that anymore. I shook my head, removed my phone from my pocket and sent a text to Gayle.

Me: *I'm at Ethan's. He's making me dinner.*

Gayle: *Sounds romantic. You two are spending a lot of time together.*

Me: *He's a really nice man. I can't believe someone hasn't snatched him up.*

Gayle: *Maybe he's been waiting for you.*

Me: *He's too young for me, Gayle.*

Gayle: *If you say so. He looks like a grownup to me.*

I didn't have a response to that. He was too young for me. Wasn't he?

I heard the whoosh of the sliding glass door and Ethan rejoined me. He placed the tray in his hands on the table. It included bread, salad filled bowls and plates with covered domes.

I put my phone on vibrate and joined him at the table. He opened the lid to the grill, moved our steak and vegetables to the plates and then recovered them. I took a seat and moved my napkin to my lap.

"Wow, I'm impressed. Everything looks delicious. Are you sure I'm not going to go in there and see the chef heading out the front door?" I pointed towards the house.

Ethan chuckled. "Not tonight." He took a seat. "Let's hope it's as good as it looks."

He reached for a fork. I reached for his hand and tilted my head. "Grace?"

He nodded. "Of course."

We closed our eyes and I hesitated waiting for him to say it. I opened one eye and found he still had his closed. Just when I was about to pray he found his voice and blessed the food.

We began to eat. The salad, a mix of super-greens that I recognized as Swiss chard, Bok Choy, spinach, and arugula along with shrimp, was tossed with a wonderful vinaigrette dressing that was flavored with ginger.

I shook my head as I let the flavors dance in my mouth.

"This is the best salad dressing I've ever tasted. What is it and can I get it in this country?"

"You can get it out of your own kitchen. It's homemade."

I dropped my fork. "Stop playing. You did not make this."

"I did, but I've been making it for years, so I've pretty much perfected it." He winked. "It has ginger in it. I made it with your delicate stomach in mind."

I swallowed hard. I didn't know how to take such a considerate gesture. I picked up my fork and pointed. "I want the recipe."

Ethan smiled and dropped his eyes to his food. I sensed my compliment carried more weight than it should. With all his confidence and success it never occurred to me that he needed affirmation, but of course he did; we all did.

"So," I said, "I'm not going to beat around the bush. Why don't you go to church anymore?"

Ethan coughed. Picked up his water glass and took a long sip.

I shook my head and tried to resist laughing. "I'm sorry. I wasn't trying to torpedo you."

"No," he cleared his throat. "I just, one second we were talking about salad dressing …" he paused, stood and escaped inside the house.

I sat back against my chair. That might have been a little rude, but he wasn't going to be wining and dining me and asking me to open my mouth and I not know if the man had gone to Africa and converted to Islam. I might not go to church every time the door opened, but I was a Christian and that wasn't changing.

I raised my glass, swirled the water around and took a

sip. Ethan came back out of the house and took a seat.

"I was about to come in and perform the Heimlich maneuver on you."

"No need. I had to check on something in the kitchen."

I squinted curiously suspecting he was actually running from my question.

His eyes widened at my questioning glare. "Okay, I confess I burned dessert."

"Oh," I said with a laugh.

"I meant to restart my timer. It's okay, I have a backup."

I laughed again and put more salad in my mouth.

He moved his salad to the side and reached for a roll. "You're laughing at me. I can't do everything right."

I returned my glass to the table. "You're so cocky. Who says you do everything right?"

Ethan took in a deep breath. A devilish look came over his face. "I'm not going to incriminate myself by answering that."

I rolled my eyes. This conversation had gone to the far side. It was time to reel it in. "That was a nice blessing you said for the food. I was asking you why you don't go to church."

Ethan reached for his glass. "What makes you think I don't go to church?"

I decided not to keep my source a secret. "Janette told me you hadn't been to Pastor Wright's church since high school."

Ethan smiled. "So, you're talking about me, eh?"

I blushed again, but resisted the urge to avert my eyes.

"I go to worship all the time. I just don't go when I'm

here."

"Why?"

"I have my reasons."

He seemed uncomfortable with the question, but I wasn't dropping this line of questioning. I had to know. "When you say worship are you talking about a Christian worship or some other kind?"

Ethan's expression became serious. "We all serve the same God don't we?"

My stomach dropped and so did my jaw.

Ethan laughed. "I'm sorry. I couldn't resist." He continued to laugh. "I'm Team Jesus forever. I just don't go to Pastor Wright's church and I don't want to embarrass him by visiting another one."

Okay, so there was some family business I didn't know anything about. Terrance hadn't mentioned strife with Ethan when we were dating. I cleared my throat like you did right before you were going to ask a nosy question. "Do you mind me asking why?"

"I don't mind you asking, but I don't really want to talk about it," he replied.

I was starting to feel like a hypocrite. I kept insisting I wouldn't date a younger man, so it shouldn't have mattered what he was or if he was still dating that model or if he was getting on a plane to God knows where the morning after the wedding. None of that should have mattered, because he was too young for me. But even with all that rationalization, I couldn't let it go. "You can't say something like that and not tell me why. I promise I won't tell a soul."

It was Ethan that cleared his throat this time. I could see he was uncomfortable. "I kind of have… had a problem with my uncle."

I tilted my head toward him indicating I needed more.

"I found a letter my mother wrote to him. I figured out I was eleven based on the postmark. She asked him if she could come back to Garrison. She wanted to live in this house." He paused. "I asked him about it, specifically why she never came and he said he told her there were conditions. No boyfriends, she had to go to church, get a job and attend drug treatment meetings. I don't think she liked the rules."

This was much heavier than I thought. I fingered the cross that hung around my neck and prayed for the right words to say to him. "Pastors always have rules," I said easily. "It's kind of a job requirement."

He inhaled deeply and then let his breath out in an audible sigh. "I know, but, she was his sister. He knew she was troubled. And it wasn't like she was going to be in his house. She wanted to stay in her father's house, but my uncle had the keys, so he had the control."

I was shocked. This story was getting worse. Ethan slumped in his chair and I was certain his posture was consistent with the way he was probably feeling.

"It's taken me ten years to stop being angry about it." He picked up his fork and played with it nervously. "It's hard for me to not think if she'd been here in Garrison that she wouldn't have died or at least she wouldn't have died before I saw her alive again."

His eyes began to shine in the dim light and my heart broke for him. I reached for his hand and squeezed it. He sat up, shook his head like he was shaking off pain. "I've never told anyone that," he said and then he shoved a piece of bread in his mouth.

"You needed to." I squeezed his hand again.

"Yeah, I guess, but it hurts to say it. Heck, it hurts to

think about it." He let out another long sigh. "And Terrance didn't help."

My ears perked up. "What did Terrance do?"

"I was upset about the conversation I had with his father. I tried to talk to him and he took up for his dad." He shook his head. "The thing is I wasn't looking for someone to agree or disagree with me. I know my mother had issues. I just wanted a listening ear. He started throwing all kinds of scripture and church rules at me." He pushed his body up in the seat and raised an eyebrow. "What did you ever see in that guy?"

We both laughed. I shook my head. "I don't know, but, I'm not trying to figure it out now."

"Well, anyway, now you know why I haven't been to my uncle's church."

Silence filled the space for a minute while we continued to eat. I had experienced a lot of pain, but this was a kind of loss I didn't know anything about. I was out of comforting words, but I couldn't not say anything. "You know your uncle has regrets too, even if he feels he made the right decision, he still has regrets. There's no way he couldn't."

Ethan raised his glass. "And he should."

I took a deep breath before my next words. "No matter what you think your uncle did you know you need to forgive him, right?"

The smile dropped from Ethan's face. He finished chewing the food in his mouth before speaking. "I already have. I'm stepping into his church for the wedding. He'll know what that means."

"Forgiveness, man style?" I asked, smiling.

"Most definitely different from the way you women do it."

We smiled at each other. Our fingers were still intertwined. He turned my hand over, examining it and rubbing the fingertips and palm until he reached my wrist. "So, tell me, did my transparency earn me some cool points?"

I slowly pulled my hand out of his. The way he touched it was so sensual that it unnerved me. I lowered my gaze and reached for bread, determined not to say the wrong thing just because everything felt right.

"I don't get an answer to that?" he asked.

I stopped being coy and met his stare. The look in his eyes was more than a little serious. I wanted to tell him he was on overload on the cool points, but I couldn't. Not in this intimate setting.

He drummed his fingers on the table and said, "Okay." I could tell it was not okay. He stood and gathered our salad dishes. "I'm going to take dessert out of the frig, so it can warm up a bit while we eat dinner."

I opened my mouth to say something to his back, but I let the protest die on my lips. He was disappointed. I didn't know what to do about that. This wasn't a date. It was dinner between friends. I was trying to keep it that way, but Ethan was pushing hard and I didn't know what he wanted. Sex? Some casual fling while he was in town? He was fine, but he wasn't fine enough for me to lose my mind and sleep with him.

I was glad to find out he wasn't backslidden, but he was still seven years younger than me and he was more than a little bit of a globetrotter. I wasn't going to be a fool. Ethan Wright was not a man who could be pinned down and I was not a woman who took flight. We weren't right for each other and I wasn't going to let a romance in Garrison break my heart. I'd been there and done that.

Chapter 9

My sleep was troubled. I tossed and turned over how I was leading Ethan on. Still I was glad to see his truck pull in the driveway, because I was two seconds from putting my hand around Janette's throat. She was such an overly dramatic princess about everything – her cow ankles that she'd named cankles, her sore breast, her weight and her pre-wedding jitters. Terrance had no idea what he signed on for. I would have to put up with her whining and complaining for a little more than a week, Terrance for life. But that was his problem, not mine. He wanted to date his ex's sister. Well, he had her. Maybe the best revenge was letting people live with their choices.

I grabbed my bag and made my way out to the truck. Ethan was waiting next to the passenger side door for me. He opened it, I climbed in and he joined me. "You look like you've eaten some nails," he said.

"It's Janette. I've had my fill of her."

"It's only eight a.m."

"It doesn't take much with my sister." I pulled my seat belt around me.

"You want to talk about it?"

"Not at all," I replied. "Let's get going."

I took in his look through my peripheral vision. He and I were dressed alike in jeans and tee-shirts. He also sported a crocheted skull cap patterned as a soccer ball. He looked cool and of course handsome. It didn't take much for him. Sex appeal oozed from his pores.

I caught him looking at my feet, or more aptly, he was staring at my leopard printed pony ankle boots.

"I can walk in these for twenty hours," I declared, raising a leg and wiggling my foot.

"Does the red bottom guy make any shoes that don't have ten inch heels?"

"The red bottom guy is Christian Louboutin," I said to be clear. "Yes, he makes flats, but I'm not sure what the point is when he designs such amazing stilettos." I smiled and put my foot down. "I thought you liked my heels."

"I do, but hey, we're shopping. I'm a practical guy," he said and then mumbled, "I'm not trying to carry you all day either."

I laughed. "Don't worry. My heels are an extension of my legs."

He shook his head and started the engine. "They're your feet, babe. Address please. I like to use my navigation when I'm in riding with a pretty lady. Cool points stay up if I don't get lost."

I gave him the side eye and then nodded toward the navigation system. "You must wear out the computer on those things."

He chuckled. "She's got jokes this morning. This truck stays in Garrison, so not many women have been in it."

I wasn't taking that bait. It was too early to talk about his love life. I read off the address and watched as he programmed the fancy buttons on the dash and we pulled out of the driveway. "It's amazing the technology we have now. I'm waiting for the day when the Jetsons reality comes to fruition. You know, cars driving themselves."

Ethan shrugged. "I'm sure somebody out there is working on it, but I won't buy. I love to get behind the wheel of a car."

"I wish I felt the same. I dread it," I said, anticipating

impending nausea. I'd forgotten to pick up motion sickness meds yesterday.

I noticed his brow knit over his eye. "Car travel is kind of a weird phobia. I remember you were in college when you finally passed the driver test. Terrance was relieved. He was sick of being your personal driver's ed. teacher."

"I was sick of him too. He was a horrible teacher." The thought of those lessons made me roll my neck.

"I couldn't wait to get my license. Driving was a rite of passage. Why so late for you?"

I propped an elbow on the window frame and rested my head against my fist. "I don't know. I've always been car sick for as long as I can remember. I wasn't looking forward to driving."

"Some people are like that," he said. "You ever try to figure out why?"

I shook my head, feeling suddenly claustrophobic about the conversation. "You don't mind if we change the subject."

Ethan nodded and silence filled the car. I sensed he was giving me time with my emotions, time to get used to the ride; time to decompress from the tense morning with Janette, but it wasn't long before we began chatting again. Ethan shared fantastic stories about life in African villages where he had gone to build homes and schools. The most interesting part was about how he slept in structures that were a little more than tents and they had water shortages and no electricity for large hunks of time during the day.

"Sounds like a different world." I tried to imagine what it must be like.

"In some respects it is, but the people want the same things we want here. Water, jobs, medical care. They want a house to come to at the end of the day and safe, clean schools for their children. Human needs and wants are universal."

"I guess I never thought about it. The work you do is so deep and important. I'm starting to feel self-conscious about the fact that I help people plan the most excessive day of their lives."

"Don't compare the two. What you do is important. Those memories of the wedding day last forever. Just because it's not life saving doesn't mean it's not life changing."

I bit down on my bottom lip and stole a peripheral glace at him. "That was deep."

"I'm a deep guy."

"Not your average jock."

"I try never to be average." He laughed heartily.

Words that were meant to stay in my head escaped from my mouth. "I've always known that."

Ethan paused a moment and then asked, "How could you? I was still a kid when you graduated from college."

"But I could tell you were mature. I remember thinking how nice it was that you turned out so great after your mom left you to –" I stopped myself. I wanted to insert an entire wedding cake in my mouth.

"It's okay. You can say it. It is what it is. After my mother ran off with a boyfriend and killed herself taking drugs." His voice came down an octave. He tightened his grip on the steering wheel. "I accepted my mother's choices a long time ago and the older I get the more I understand that that's all we can do. Wishing it was different doesn't change it and not talking about it doesn't make it disappear."

"Still I didn't mean to bring your mother up again. We just talked about her last night."

"It's cool." He cast a glance at me. "We're both orphans. It's not like you don't understand what I'm feeling."

He was right about that. I'd had much more than he did, because at least I had my father. "You can't stop the people you love from having time in your head. I believe you can control your thoughts, take captive every one and bring it under submission… just like it says in the Bible, but I think about my parents every day whether I want to or not."

Ethan raised his hand to his chest and pointed an index finger at his heart. "That's because they're in here. They're not just in our heads. I like to believe that the good part of them stays with us."

I smiled. We had been silent for a few minutes when I continued, "I can't stop wondering how different I would have been if I'd been raised in a house with a woman in it."

Ethan let go of the steering wheel and took the hand that was closest to him. "Well, if it means anything to you, I can't imagine that you'd be any more perfect than you are now."

I looked at him and he took his eyes off the road for a second and caught mine.

I squeezed his hand. "Thanks for saying that. You have no idea how much it means right now.'

"Don't second guess yourself. You're amazing. I know that it might be hard with your sister marrying your ex and all, but still…Terrance wasn't the right man for you anyway."

"I always thought he was. The only reason we broke up was because I wouldn't stay in Garrison and he wouldn't leave."

"No, it's not. You think it is, but if you were meant to be together somebody would have caved. You would've set up shop in Atlanta or he would've found something to do up north. You just weren't meant to be together."

I sighed. "So you think he and Janette are?"

"I don't know. I don't know anything about what they've got going on, but they seem happy together."

A part of me wanted to believe that. The part that loved my sister, but still Terrance's behavior was questionable. "If they're so happy, why is he swinging at you?"

Ethan chuckled. "He's wanted to hit me for years. It has nothing to do with you."

"Somehow I don't believe that's it," I said, looking out the window and taking in the beautiful fall colors that decorated the trees.

"Maybe you need to ask him."

I closed my eyes and hugged my arms to my chest. "I'm afraid of what he'll say."

"Come again." Ethan gave me a quick glance.

I sighed loudly. "It's weird. I want him to marry my sister because she's pregnant, but then again, I don't. I want him to love her not just be obligated to her. Marriages that begin like that seldom work."

"Janette's a big girl. She knows what she's getting herself into. Have you talked to her about it?"

"No. I don't like to talk to her about the marriage."

"You're planning the wedding."

"Yeah, and that and a marriage are two different things."

Ethan tightened his grip on the steering wheel again. I knew he was about to say something deep. "Go the distance, big sis and do what you came here to do. Make sure your little sister is okay."

He delivered the depth I was anticipating. I sighed and nodded. He was right. If I was going to be here the least I could do is what I said I would do. "How did you get to be so wise for a youngster?"

"Age ain't nothin' but a number, babe." He cast a glance my way and winked. "I keep telling you that."

I slapped his arm. "You are so…I don't even know."

"Irresistible." He laughed and the sound made me feel all warm inside. It was unnerving and seemingly stronger than the nausea, because I hadn't felt sick the entire ride.

***

We arrived at our first location where I was planning to get the majority of the items I needed. Last night, I decided to go with the first thing that came to mind when she told me fuchsia was her color. The wedding would have a "Blissful Pink" theme. A mix of soft and vibrant colors, traditional, yet fun. The reception hall would be decorated with hanging miniature lights and large flowers displays. We'd have traditional place settings and place cards and candles, but we'd make it fun with a cotton candy stand for wedding favors and we'd light sparklers for the exit rather than throw confetti or rice. The vision of the event came to me in a flood of images. It was like a dam was unlocked. I was going to be in the zone from now until she said I do.

Ethan and I hit a few other stores, but we couldn't find everything I needed. I didn't have time to order. I was disappointed and he sensed it.

"Where do you usually get this kind of stuff?"

"E-commerce stores. That's the way it's done these days. There's a brick and mortar shop in Mason, North Carolina. I could place an order, but even if I put a rush on it, there's no guarantee I'll have it in time for the wedding."

"What's Mason near?"

"It's a small city halfway between Fayetteville and Wilmington."

Ethan was thoughtful for a few seconds. "That's an easy spot to get to. We should go there."

"Go to Mason?" Just thinking about that long drive brought on nausea. "It's too far."

"We could fly."

"And how would we get everything back? It's bound to be too heavy to check in baggage claim."

"It won't be if it's the only baggage."

I was perplexed and he read my expression. He removed his phone from his pocket and raised a finger to quiet me while he dialed.

"Hey Keith. Yeah, I'm still here. Look, if you're not taking her up today, I need to borrow your plane. Sure. Okay, okay. I got it. Yes. Right now." He ended the call and returned his phone to his pocket. "Okay, sweetheart. We're going to Mason."

I was still perplexed, so he continued. "I have a friend that owns a plane. It's at Atlanta Regional airport. We're borrowing it."

"Are you serious?"

"I just made the call."

"Who's the pilot?"

"I am. I've flown it dozen times or so."

I shook my head. "I can't. Don't take it personally, but I don't really like to fly."

"Fly. Drive. We're going to work on that today." He grabbed my arm. "Come on."

I resisted by parking by heels. "No, you don't

understand. You'll be wearing my lunch."

"I get you, but this is important to you so you'll face your fears and get your work done."

I continued to protest. "I don't want to face my fear today."

"Yes you do," he said opening the truck door. "Get in."

By the time we arrived at Atlanta Regional Airport, I was as green as Ethan's truck. "I can't."

"You can," Ethan replied.

"I don't want to," I insisted. "And besides, I have a rule about planes. No tiny ones."

"You have a rule," he guffawed. "Why am I not surprised?"

We were at a standoff. "You're doing this today, Nectar. I've got my own reasons for wanting you to get over this car and plane thing, but we'll talk about that at another time. Let's switch places."

"Now? In the truck?"

"Yep." He opened his door and jumped out. Then he came around to my side and opened the door for me. Reluctantly, I climbed down and claimed the driver's seat. Ethan closed the door behind me and jumped in where I had been.

"Okay. Start it," he ordered.

I did as I was told and just like always sickness rose from my belly.

"What are you feeling?"

"You mean other than car sick?"

"Describe your exact symptoms."

"I feel a little nausea. Warm like I could start perspiring.

Just ill. It's called car sickness."

"You're not feeling car sick, Nectar. The car isn't in motion."

I glared at him curiously. "The car doesn't have to be in motion."

"Yeah, it does, because being car sick is a kind of motion sickness."

I shrugged. "I'm anticipating it."

He shook his head. "I don't think so."

"You know so much then what is it?"

He bit his lips and drummed a finger on his knee. After few moments he said, "I think you know."

Silence enveloped the vehicle for a long time. I gripped the steering wheel and started straight ahead. Every time I turned my head to look at Ethan his eyes compelled me to go where I didn't want to go emotionally. I did know what it was, but I had never talked about it, not until now. "The car accident."

"I'm no therapist, but that's what I'm guessing." He reached for my hand, peeled the one closest to him off the wheel and gave it a tight squeeze. "Tell me about it."

I hesitated. Tears filled my eyes. I took a deep breath before speaking. "I was in the car with her when she was killed. I was in the back seat of course. I don't remember it that clearly. Just the bang. My mom not answering me when I cried. The police and the ambulance."

Ethan nodded. I hadn't talked about that day in a long time. I felt a sharp pain, but it wasn't in my body, it was a jab in my soul. Ethan squeezed my hand. "It's never occurred to you that that might be why you get sick in a car?"

I shook my head. "Not really." I blinked back tears. "I get sick on planes too. She didn't die in a plane crash, so I can't see what it has to do with planes."

He shrugged. "It might not be about the car. It could be the loss of control."

I nodded. "Control." I'd thought this myself. I always had to control everything and I knew that wasn't a good thing. Gayle had even suggested I see a therapist. "How do I get over it? I mean short of visiting a shrink."

"Well therapy isn't a terrible thing. I had to see someone after I hurt my knee. We talked about a whole lot of stuff besides my knee."

I appreciated him being brave enough to share that with me, but I wasn't sure how the plan would work today and I said so. "How's it going to help me with this plane ride?"

"I'm going to be therapy for you. You pray and squeeze my hand every time you feel bad."

I chuckled through tears, opened my bag and removed a tissue. "You're going to be bruised."

He reached for a fallen tendril of my hair and tucked it behind my ear. "But you'll be better." He lowered his hand to my chin, tipped it up and planted a kiss on my forehead. "That's all that matters."

I took a deep breath and opened the door. "Let's do this."

Chapter 10

The flight from Atlanta to Fayetteville was nearly painless. For the thirty minutes I gripped Ethan's hand every couple of minutes. When he was using both hands I clutched his upper arm and grabbed onto his knee. I was a wreck. Ethan squeezed my hand back and spoke comforting words that took my mind off the fact that I was in a small plane and had absolutely no control over the circumstances. I said some prayers that helped, but most of it was my resolve to not get sick and Ethan's resolve to help me through it. We made a great team.

Ethan rented a car at the airport. Using GPS, we made it to the store with two hours to spare before closing time, but we found a sign on the door that read: *Closed for family emergency. Will reopen in the morning.*

I stood on my tip toes and leaned against the glass door to look in. "No way. We suffered through all that for nothing?"

Ethan peeked in the glass also. "What are we looking for?" he asked. "A miracle?"

I groaned. "I can't believe we came all this way for nothing."

"It wasn't a total waste. You're over your fear of small planes."

"But I still don't have the stuff I need for Janette's wedding." I dropped my head back. "This isn't good."

Ethan put a hand on my shoulder. "Don't stress. We'll come back in the morning."

I fell into step next to him as we walked back to the rental car. "You mean stay overnight?"

He pushed the key fob for the locks and opened my door. "We'll check into a hotel, eat some dinner and relax."

I decided not to buck at that idea. This store was really the place I needed for my list and it was so generous of him to offer.

We climbed back in the SUV and drove to a Holiday Inn Express we'd passed coming into town. Ethan put the car in park and hopped out." He was only inside for a minute. "It's full."

We pulled back on the road and stopped at another hotel and then another and another. They were all full. Finally, the last hotel in town had one room.

"Why aren't there any rooms in this town?" I asked the desk clerk.

"There's a convention for the direct sellers association. The only reason we have this room is because someone became ill and checked out an hour ago."

Lucky for us I guess, but then realized Ethan and I had to share. "What kind of room is it?" I asked hoping it was a suite big enough to sleep a family of ten.

"It's a King." The clerk replied.

"One bed?"

"And a sofa sleeper," he added.

I sighed. "That's not going to work."

Ethan shot a glance in my direction and passed the clerk a credit card. "We'll take it." I gave him the side eye and he threw up his hands. "I'm not sleeping in the rental car."

We had dinner at a burger restaurant across the street from the hotel, picked up a change of clothes and some toiletries at the local Target and headed back to our hotel.

We entered the room and both stopped near the door

and stared at the lone bed.

"Oh my God," I murmured.

"You don't need God. I'm only twenty-nine, so your rule will keep you."

I smacked his arm.

He laughed. "Seriously, I'm on the couch and I'll be the perfect gentleman."

"Are you capable of that?"

He put his hands on both my shoulders. "I think I've proven myself to be more than capable. The question is are you?"

My heart was beating out of my chest. I didn't say what I was thinking, which was *I hope so.* I looked toward the restroom, desperate for a way to separate myself from him already. The room was large, but shrinking by the second. "Ladies first?"

"Ladies first in all things," he replied. I didn't miss the subtle, yet suggestive change in his tone.

What a player.

Once in the restroom, I showered, slid on the two piece lounge set I'd purchased and brushed my teeth.

I found Ethan on the balcony. I understood why he was out there. The sun was setting. The skyline was beautiful.

"Can I join you?" I asked, stepping out.

He turned to me, gave me a visual sweep from head to toe and replied, "I'd like nothing better."

"Is that the Cape Fear River?" I asked, admiring the large bridge that provided the backdrop for the rainbow of orange, yellow and brown hues that decorated the sky.

"Yep, and that's the Memorial Bridge."

My peripheral vision indicated he was facing me. I turned my head and glanced at him. He did another head to toe sweep and licked his lips. I was starting to feel like the dessert he'd opted to skip at the restaurant. I think he sensed my discomfort because he took a few steps away from me and turned back to face the view.

"You smell good," he said. His voice had taken on a husky quality.

I avoided looking in his direction. So that was it. The shower gel was working on his senses. I clutched the railing and swallowed hard. Sharing a hotel room was a bad idea.

"Watching the sun set is my favorite thing to do." Ethan perched an arm on the balcony railing and turned toward me again. "Well, one of them."

Pulse pounding I let our eyes connect again. "You are not behaving yourself, Ethan Wright."

That devilish glint returned to his eyes. He chuckled. "What did I do?"

"You know what you're doing. You're flirting way too much and all this sexual innuendo. Stop playing with me."

Ethan laughed hard. "Okay, I'm just being myself. I'm sorry." He paused. "I admit its fun to tease you."

I squared my shoulders. "Let's get back to what we were talking about. You love sunsets. What are the others?" I asked. I really was curious about what a man like him liked to do, but I cast a warning glare in his direction. "Keep it clean."

"Okay, you have to remember I'm a simple country boy, so don't look for anything super interesting." He raised his hands, clasped them together over his head and stretched. That move made his perfectly sculpted abs ripple. I had to fight to keep from staring. "If you're going to make me expose myself I hope I'm going to get the same from you."

His lazy, knowing smile made me wonder if I'd fought staring at his abs hard enough.

I felt my face flush. I wasn't committing myself. I nodded. "Go on."

"You already know I enjoy flying. Horseback riding. I love the beach…even in the winter. I like to go for long car rides. I like to stay up late at night watching old movies like Cape Fear. It's one of my favorites. I like to cook Italian food. I even know how make pasta by hand."

I was impressed with his list. It was so romantic that I wanted to disappear in it.

"But," he added, "my second favorite thing to do in the whole world is work with kids."

"Really?" I remembered how great he was with that child in Palermo's.

"I'm nuts about them. They're much more fun than adults. Anyway, I'm working on a business plan to open fitness centers for kids."

I raised an eyebrow. "Really, kids working out?"

"There's an obesity crisis. You'll remember I was a chunky kid."

"I do, but you started playing sports. Isn't that what kids should do?"

"Maybe, but everybody doesn't like sports. I don't recall you ever playing one," he said, "And most kids don't like playing outside alone. If their neighbors are inside moving their thumbs across a game controller or surfing the internet, what's a kid to do?"

"Interesting. I guess when you don't have children, you don't think about their challenges. Fitness centers for kids. I've never heard of that."

"Good, I'd like to think of myself as a pioneer." He

smiled. "Anyway, it would work well in urban areas. We'd also teach the kids about nutrition. Very few schools still have home economics programs, so we'd offer some cooking classes too. It would be kind of an afterschool recreation center with a twist."

"It's brilliant."

"I thought so."

Our eyes caught and we held our gazes for a moment. I broke the stare with a question. "Are you trying to get federal grant money?"

"Not initially. Maybe once I prove my model."

I smiled.

"You like?" he asked.

"I'm impressed. Have you decided where you want to put the first one?"

"Kind of. It's going to depend on some things."

"Like?"

He zipped his finger across his lips. "I've revealed enough. Now it's your turn."

"You said working with kids was number two. What's number one?"

That devilish look flashed across his face again. "I promised to keep it G-rated."

I smirked. "I guess I walked into that one."

"Yes you did." He took my hand. Don't worry I've cleaned up my act in that department.

"So, you're saying you're celibate."

"I think so," Ethan replied, smiling slyly. "Anway, I don't want to even get near the conversation of sex right now." He paused. "And don't think I haven't noticed that we're still talking about me. It's time for you to share."

"I'm not near as interesting."

"I find that hard to believe." His voice had gotten husky again, too husky for two people sharing a room.

"Well," I replied allowing my eyes to lock with his. "I –" My cell phone rang. "Let me make sure that's not Janette."

I stepped back through the door and followed the ring to my phone. A picture of Janette's face flashed on the screen, so I answered. "Hey how are…what? When?"

I heard Ethan come in and the balcony door closing behind him.

"No, that's horrible. Yes, I know, but try not to upset yourself, remember you're watching your stress." I listened to her go on a bit more and then interrupted her wailing. "Yes, Janette but these things happen. Don't worry. It's my job. I'll take care of it." Ethan placed his hands on my shoulders. He began to gently massage as if he knew I needed it. "No," I turned toward him. "I won't be back tonight. I told you. Yes, I'm…Janette, let me do the job you asked me to do. Okay, goodbye."

I ended the call, turned in Ethan's direction and dropped my head back for a moment.

"What is it?"

"The caterer had a fire. The entire place burned down. All their equipment is damaged."

Ethan whistled. "Wow, that's messed up."

"Yes, messed up for them and me. I've got no food." I grabbed my handbag and pulled out my iPad. "I'll have to see what else I can come up with."

"Now? It's eight p.m. at night"

"It's actually not a horrible time. I'll try a few restaurants that do catering. The manager or assistant manager would still be there. The dinner rush is over, so they'll be able to talk." I tapped on the app that held my Atlanta restaurant contacts. "I had a list of backups I can start with. I might be able to get the preliminaries out of the way." I sat down and pulled up my list.

"Anything I can do?" Ethan asked.

I looked up at him. He was doing a good job hiding it, but I could tell he was disappointed.

"No," I replied. "I need to start making calls."

He nodded. "I'm going to go down to the gym." He swiped his room key off the desk and walked out.

I sighed. I didn't like disappointing him, but it was for the best that we were interrupted. We were getting too close. This was a business trip, not a getaway. We were stuck here because my vendor had an emergency. I wasn't going to let it turn into some kind of romantic excursion, lose my head over this gorgeous hunk of a man, and let him discard me as easily as he did an old pair of soccer cleats by hopping on the first plane headed for Africa. I was already nursing a bruised ego from all this wedding business. I didn't need a broken heart.

Broken heart. Had I just thought that? I'd been in town four days and hadn't seen Ethan in five years. I was not falling in love. He was just fine and sexy and smart and cultured and interesting and attentive and…Oh God! He was too much. I shook my head, sighed again and picked up my phone to call the first restaurant on my list. I needed to focus on work, so I could get the thought of Ethan flexing his muscles downstairs in the gym out of my mind.

***

The next morning I felt a cool breeze blowing from Ethan's direction. Last night I'd made a few calls and jumped into bed before he returned from the gym. He showered for a long time, opened the pullout sofa, and crashed. I'd listened to him toss and turn all night. I felt horrible about it. I hoped that his exhaustion wouldn't affect his ability to fly the plane and get us back to Atlanta safely, but I knew I had to take the bed because there was no way he was going to let me sleep on the sofa. I couldn't invite him into the bed because even though it was king sized it would not be big enough for the two of us.

I was determined to remain celibate until I got married. Every person really trying to live a celibate life knew you never put yourself into situations where temptation might get the better of you. Ethan was some serious temptation. Sharing the room was bad enough. We could not sit up talking into the night becoming more and more interested in each other.

I'd felt sure about my decision, but now looking at the angry set of his jaw across the breakfast table I realized I'd done him a wee bit wrong. I hadn't had to handle things the way I had. The man had driven me into the city, helped me shop, borrowed his friend's plane, driven around to hotels so I could stay overnight and finish doing what I needed to do and what had I offered him in return? Fake snoring. I shouldn't have pretended. I could have explained how I felt. I sighed heavily. I didn't know what else to do. I needed to keep our relationship where it needed to stay…in the friend zone.

After breakfast we checked out of the hotel and headed to "Weddings and More". We arrived ten minutes before the store opened. I couldn't stand Ethan's sour disposition, so I opted to escape the chill in the car.

"I'm going to wait outside." I pointed in the direction of a bench in front of the store. I thought Ethan was going a bit overboard in the pissed off department, but still, I had a big "G" for guilty on my forehead. He probably knew I was faking sleep when he came in last night.

After five minutes of reading a book on the Kindle app on my phone Ethan joined me on the bench. "Did you find a caterer?" he asked. His jaw line was noticeably softer. I guess he'd tossed my sins into the sea of forgetfulness.

"I might have," I replied. "It's a popular restaurant in Atlanta. The price isn't bad and they have a good reputation."

"So, what do you have to do to get the deal done?"

"They'll give me a call this afternoon to let me know if they can accommodate us. If it's a yes, I'll probably drive in tomorrow and sample some of the items on the menu."

Ethan rested his back against the bench and stretched his arm across the back of it. "You don't want to do that today?"

I hesitated, refused to look him in the eye. "I didn't want to ask you for anything else."

"I don't mind. I like," he paused, "…I don't have anything else planned today."

I didn't respond. The "G" that had been on my forehead was now over my mouth.

"We'll already be in the city, so –" he paused again. "Look, Nectar, I'm sorry about last night."

The shock I felt had to show on my face. I was the one who had done him wrong. "Sorry about what?"

"Sorry that I was trying to turn our down time into an opportunity."

I raised an eyebrow, curiously. "An opportunity?"

"To get to know you better. You've been pretty clear

that you're not interested in me, and I keep pushing."

I opened my mouth to speak, but I wasn't sure what to say that wouldn't contradict what I'd been saying.

"I'm cool with us being friends. I can't expect you to break all your rules just because I want you to. Rules are in place for a reason right?" he smiled, but it didn't reach his eyes.

I hesitated and replied, "Right."

"Plus, I didn't even ask you if you involved in a relationship. Kind of presumptuous of me to assume that you're not."

I shook my head. "Ethan."

The closed sign in the window was flipped over to open and we could hear keys in the locks.

"Really, I got the message last night," he said. "You go do your shopping. I'm going to browse in some of the stores." He stood and walked away.

We were obviously not cool, because yesterday he seemed to enjoy helping me pick out every item I needed and didn't seem to mind the painstaking process.

I stood just as the shop door opened.

"Good morning," the shopkeeper said. She removed the handwritten note about the early closing. "How nice to open the door to a customer."

I swallowed the disappointment of not having Ethan with me, put on my game face and introduced myself. The woman was the owner and she recognized me from all the e-commerce business I had given her over the years. We made some small talk about the industry and then about my upcoming event and proceeded to fill my shopping cart. The owner knew her inventory, which made the process go quickly, but it wasn't nearly as fun as it had been yesterday when I was explaining to Ethan what the various items I was picking out were for. By the time she and I were done, I had all the items I needed to create the perfect setting for the sanctuary and reception hall. Tulle, tea lights, a fuchsia floor runner, candy tins, ribbon, the list of items was nearly endless.

She and I closed the trunk on the rental SUV just as Ethan exited a store down the street. "All set?" he asked, opening the passenger side door so I could slip in.

"Yes." I noticed he didn't have any bags. "You didn't find anything while you were shopping."

He shrugged. "Nothing I couldn't get in Atlanta. I was just killing time."

Just putting distance between us, I thought.

We made the forty minute trip to the airport. To Ethan's credit, he did ask me about my purchases and genuinely seemed interested in my finds. He also told me a cute story about an elderly couple in the bookstore.

"I love to read," he said as he wrapped it up. "One day I'm going to find a woman who likes to read too and we'll lie in hammocks in our backyard and read to each other."

OMG! Was he for real or was this man so good at running game?

"Sounds like a nice afternoon, right?" he asked.

I swallowed. "It does. I'm guessing that hammock is hanging up in Argentina or Africa somewhere?"

"It'll be where ever she wants it to be. I've seen the world. I can settle down," he said. "For the right woman."

"I'm told every man settles down for the right woman."

"You've heard that right. If a man won't make a serious commitment then he's not serious about the woman."

"So does that explain why you broke that supermodel's heart last year? What was her name? Concei?"

"Concei and I had a great relationship. She just wasn't the woman I wanted to spend the rest of my life with. I'm not setting myself up for drama. I don't care how fine she is."

"But you can date her?" I said, gruffly.

"Uh, yeah, I can definitely do that," he chuckled. "You know all of my business, because the paparazzi are taking pictures. I still don't know if you have a man."

I reached for my soft drink and took a sip. "I'm not seeing anyone right now."

I stole a glance at him. He nodded and raised an eyebrow. "It's a shame I'm so young, because I make a really nice boyfriend." He turned off the rental car and climbed out.

I pressed my head against the window and sighed deeply. My instincts told me he was telling the truth about that, but I had no idea what I was supposed to do about it.

Chapter 11

Janette's bridal shower was held in our backyard on late Sunday afternoon. We decided to do a barbeque since the weather was forecast to be gorgeous. The caterer provided chopped barbeque pork and chicken and yummy side items that included potato salad, macaroni and cheese, baked beans and a few other casseroles and vegetables. I'd ordered a cupcake tower from the bakery and it turned out beautiful. They'd created ten different designs of white and dark pink cupcakes and filled the centers with raspberry colored pudding. We served dark pink colored drinks – lemonade, sangria and even tinted the Sprite.

I rented a huge canopy and decorated it with fresh pink heather and used white taffeta as a drape. It served as the place for Janette's chaise, which the girls and I covered, in a glittery fuchsia fabric. We strung tiny gold lights through the canopy and across the back of the chair.

The decorations were beautiful. Unable to contain her joy, Janette stepped out of the house and burst into tears. The makeup she'd spent so much time making perfect for the pictures was ruined.

Mother Wright and I stood near the rear end of the canopy enjoying Janette's reaction. "If this is what you do for a shower I can't imagine what you have in store for the wedding."

"The plans are gorgeous. Hopefully we can pull it off," I replied.

Mother Wright took my hand. "I'm sure you'll far exceed the idea you have on paper." She smiled at me. "You know, I always thought you'd be my daughter-in-law."

I took a deep breath and shook my head. "Not meant to

be, apparently."

"But I wasn't wrong. I know my son. You were close."

"We were," I said with a nod of my head.

"Terrance can be private, but I sensed a deep heartache when you left after your father's funeral."

"I think it was a hard time for both of us. We realized that we weren't going to be together. I was going back to New York no matter what."

Mother Wright didn't say anything. I suspected she didn't understand a someone like me; a woman who put career ahead of marriage not when she'd sacrificed everything for her husband and children and their church.

"Janette is better suited for him," I added.

"It's not the ideal way to begin a marriage, but Lord knows they're not the first to go this way and they won't be the last. I just hope they know each other or even if they don't, that they'll find a way to work through their individualities," Mother Wright said. "My son can be stubborn."

"So can my sister, but I'm sure they'll find their way."

We were interrupted by Ethan. He squeezed between us and put an arm around both of our shoulders. "Deniece did a great job with the decorations, didn't she Auntie?"

"We were just talking about it," she replied.

"My truck was packed from front to back," he added.

"I'm sure Deniece appreciated having your help." Mother Wright swept a look between us and smiled at me. "I'm going to get some lemonade. Can I bring some for either of you?"

"I'm fine." Ethan and I both said in unison.

Mother Wright looked amused by that. She wagged a

finger and walked away.

I looked over toward the grilling area. The men had refused to be left out of the festivities. Terrance, Ethan, and a few of their friends, manned grills that smoked with the scents of steak, shrimp, chicken, hamburgers and sausage links. I was glad to see Ethan. I'd been busy, but I still missed him much more than I cared to think about.

Hands on my hips I turned to him. "I thought you were on shrimp duty. We don't want it blackened by mistake."

"I delegated," he said, authoritatively. "Leaders do that."

"Always the funny guy. So, I haven't seen you in a few days. You've been busy."

"I decided to get started on my kid's fitness center. I threw myself into the business plan."

"Is the business you and Terrance have not going to keep you busy enough?"

"I'm an investor. Terrance's going to run the day to day. I don't want to get in his way."

"So, it was all about helping your cousin?"

"And bringing some jobs to Garrison. That plant has been in trouble for years. You never know when it's going to start laying off folks. Terrance is wise to have a backup plan."

"He's always been a planner."

"I guess you two had that in common."

"Obviously that wasn't enough. We're here," I said. "I don't want to talk about my relationship with Terrance. Tell me, have you decided where you want to put the first gym?"

"No, it's up in the air."

"Is Atlanta on the short list?"

"I'm not telling."

"What about the name?"

"Working on that too."

"Two days of planning and you have no launch city and no name. What exactly have you decided?"

"It's top secret stuff, but I can share one thing I've decided over the last two days."

He stepped closer to me. I stepped back. My heart began racing. "What's that?"

His voice dropped to a husky murmur. "That I'm nuts about you. I figured that one out the other night after I dropped you off, but I was sure of it by Saturday morning."

My breath caught in my throat.

"Ethan, your break is over," Terrance called.

"I'll talk to you later." He returned to man his grill.

My heart pounded. He thought he'd missed me. My emotions had put the "m" in missed. Getting through the day without hearing his voice had been horrible. What had I done? Come to Garrison to fall in love with another unavailable man? Was I wrong to want to live in New York City and build my business? Was God trying to show me that by pulling me back here and practically beating me over the head with Ethan?

I felt so unsure about everything. Love is supposed to be something positive and right. I wasn't supposed to be this confused. But was it me? Was I making it hard for myself by questioning everything? Was I supposed to go with the flow? I didn't know how to do that. I wasn't a go with the flow type of gal. I planned everything. That's who I was.

The photographer called the women together to take some pictures before the food was served. I joined my sister and the girls under the canopy. He took some fun pictures of the group and then some shots of Janette and me.

My smile had a little more "happy" in it because of Ethan's words and then because of the look he was giving me as I posed for the camera. It was so amazing to me that he looked at me like I was the only woman out here when he'd dated so many gorgeous women over the years. I wasn't bad looking, but I was no Victoria Secret model. I hid the twenty pounds I needed to lose in my height and a good body shaper, but I knew they were there. Ethan was used to physical perfection. When he wasn't dating a model it was a female athlete. I wasn't sure how to compete with that. One could argue that I could work at losing my twenty pounds, but once you started making changes for a man it never ended. I was not going to be that girl. It was all wrong.

After the food was served, the men begged to steal a few minutes in our living room to catch the end of the football game. We ladies had cupcakes and drinks while Janette opened her gifts. She received some pretty sexy lingerie; a few gag gifts and a couple of toys that made Mother Wright blush. Claiming fatigue, Janette retired inside and the ladies and I cleaned up. The men came out, folded the chairs and put them in the back of Terrance's truck and then they cleaned their grills and rolled them onto the backs of their respective pickup trucks. Every man in Garrison had a pickup. A truck was required to keep a man card.

Ethan and Terrance were the last of the group. Janette and I were in her bedroom where I was helping her sort through her gifts.

"The shower was perfection." Janette gushed.

"The pictures are going to be amazing." I leaned against the desk.

"I can hardly wait to see what you have planned for the wedding."

I smiled. "Something fit for the sister of a wedding

planner."

"I can see why you make so much money doing what you do. If you can do this in a month, I can't imagine what you come up with when you have more funds and time."

"Most of my clients aren't rich. They're just regular people who want to stretch their money and have an amazing wedding. Sometimes it's cheaper to hire an expert than to try to do it yourself."

"I suppose," Janette said. "I know I've been to some janky DIY weddings here in Garrison. You remember the Atkins last year?"

"I remember you sending me pictures from the reception."

We both scrunched up our faces at the same time and laughed.

"I forgot about that. Must be pregnancy brain."

A beat of silence passed between us. I looked out the window to see if Ethan was still there. He and Terrance were standing in front of Terrance's truck talking."

Janette leaned forward to take a peek. "As long as they aren't rolling around in the grass."

I chuckled. "Boys will be boys."

"Especially when one of them is trying to take the other's toy."

I eyed her curiously. "What does that mean?"

"Well, you know, Terrance was trying to block on Ethan. He doesn't think his intentions are right." I didn't respond. Janette continued. "And he was right about him. It's no wonder he was so successful at playing soccer. He's good at games."

I rolled my eyes. "What's that supposed to mean?"

"He's down here trying to get with you and it seems he's dating that model, Concei, again."

I didn't want to have this conversation with my sister, but I was too curious not to ask, "What would make you say that?"

"An interview she had that I read this morning." Janette reached for her iPad and shoved it at me. "I was going to email it to you, but since you're here."

I read the blurb that indeed said that Ethan Wright would be attending an annual fundraiser event as her escort. A lump stuck in my throat and I swallowed, forcing it down. "He said they weren't seeing each other anymore."

"He probably says a lot of things to get what he wants."

I continued to stare at the article. At his name. At the pictures they posted of the couple when they were on previous red carpets events. I handed the tablet back to Janette. "It doesn't matter. We're just friends."

"Friends who fly off and stay out of town all night. Come on now. I might have been born at night, but it wasn't last night, sugah."

"Janette, nothing happened. In fact, he was the perfect gentleman. That would be something you know nothing about."

Janette's fist flew to her hips. "What's that supposed to mean?"

"I can add, Janette. You and Terrance were in bed practically on your first date. Not only wasn't he a gentleman, but you weren't much of a lady."

Janette gasped. "It wasn't the first date and here you go with Terrance again. Just because Ethan is a jerk doesn't mean you have to go passing your pain around by talking about Terrance."

I didn't say anything.

"And it's not like you wanted him. You dumped him. Twice."

I pressed my fingers to temples. Why couldn't my sister understand or at least admit she was wrong. "Whether or not I dumped him isn't really the point."

"It is the point. You're being all territorial about the man and you don't even care about him."

"And you know this because we what…broke up?"

"No, because he told me what happened. As far as I can tell, he's the one who should be feeling funny."

It was me who put my hands on my hips this time. "What do you mean he told you what happened?"

"He told me that you two talked about getting serious when daddy was sick, but then you told him that you were feeling vulnerable because you were sad and it wasn't the right time to try a relationship."

"That's what he said."

"Yes, why is there more?" Janette raised her head defiantly as if daring me to call her man a liar. I wasn't going to take the bait.

"Janette, you can be so naïve. It doesn't matter. He's your man. You believe what you want. Just try to live happily ever after because if you don't, I don't want to hear about it."

I stomped out of her room passing Terrance in the hall.

"The party was real nice –" he started.

I threw up a hand to silence him and kept moving toward the stairs. I grabbed Janette's keys off the foyer table and pushed the front door open. This house was too small for the three of us.

"Hey." I heard Ethan's voice behind me. "Where are you going?"

"I need to get away from here."

I could hear his footsteps behind me. "What happened?"

I opened Janette's car door and climbed in without answering him.

"Let me take you for a drive. You don't need to be behind the wheel this angry. You're as dangerous as a drunk."

I scowled at him and he snatched his head back.

"No thanks," I barked. "I don't need them and I don't need you."

I started the engine.

Ethan threw his arms up. "What did I do?"

"Nothing!" I barked. "You did absolutely nothing. I'll see you at the wedding." I gunned the engine and shot out of the driveway.

***

I didn't make it a mile down the road before I saw the headlights of a monster truck in my rearview mirror. I groaned. "Why can't the Wright men just leave me alone? Neither one of them really wants me, but they keep tormenting me."

I kept driving. He sped up. I sped up. He sped up again. My cell phone rang. I ignored it. It rang again. I ignored it again. He continued to follow me for ten more minutes. I was forced to pull into a gas station because the gas light came on; so much for my escape.

I climbed out of the car, reached back in for my purse and was hit with the realization that I'd left it at the house, again. I cursed under my breath. I had no money for gas.

Ethan was out of his truck, charging toward me and he was steaming. "Are you out of your mind?"

I was deceptively calm when I replied. "You were the one drag racing on the road, not me."

"I was trying to catch up with you. When you sped up, you made it racing."

I had been avoiding his eyes, but now I made contact that would have stabbed him if I could make daggers. "I thought you were smart. How did you miss the message that I didn't want to be followed?"

He arched a thumb at his chest. "Did I do something?"

Ignoring him, I turned to the car and removed the gas cap.

"You went into the house with your sister and came out like a rhinoceros on the tear."

I whipped around to face him. "Did you just call me a rhino?"

He shook his head. "I just described how you bolted out of the house."

"Like a rhino. You don't think that's a strong image to associate with me?"

"Deniece." He put his hands on my shoulders. "Please, I'm just a man. Help me here. What is going on?"

I slapped his hands away. "You're not just a man. You're a lying man and there's nothing I can do to help you with that."

Noticeably shocked, Ethan stepped back. "Lying about what?"

"Probably everything, but I don't have time to talk about it. I forgot my purse and the car is almost out of gas." I mellowed my tone a bit. "Will you loan me ten? I'll pay you back in the morning."

He folded his arms across his chest. I could tell he was relieved to have something to hold over me. "I'm not doing anything until you tell me why you're calling me a liar. I've never lied to you."

I was not going to be manipulated. Images of Concei with her long, lithe body draped around Ethan entered my mind. I groaned. He'd never say she did anything like a Rhino, but it wasn't even about her. I was hurt that he'd tried to play me. I sneered at him. "I don't need you." I stomped into the store with Ethan on my heels as I approached the counter. "Do you receive Western Union here?" I asked the clerk.

"Yes ma'am," the clerk responded.

"What do you need Western Union for?" Ethan asked.

"I'm going to have a friend send me some money for gas." I opened my contacts on my phone. I'd seen the Western Union commercials. You could send money online within minutes. Gayle would help me.

Ethan grabbed my phone. "You're acting insane. I'll gas up the car." He reached into his wallet and handed the clerk a credit card. "Fill it up on pump three."

"Thank you," I replied and stomped out of the store.

"Hold up. Will you just let me sign this receipt? I'll pump it."

I smiled as I charged toward the pump station. I was determined to get my own gas started before he could finish up at the register. I didn't expect him to be so fast. I had my hand on the nozzle. He reached for it. I raised it over my head and he leaned into me, pushing my body flush against the car. Our faces were within inches of each other. I could feel his breath coming hard from the run he's just made out of the store. I burned him with the heat of my stare, but instead of discouraging him, he put his lips on mine. I squirmed, fighting with one hand. Ethan reached up for the gas nozzle, took it from me and put his other free hand behind my head and continued to kiss me. I used the force of both my arms to push his body away from mine.

"You don't get to do that!"

The heat of his glare intensified. "Do what? Kiss you? Want you?"

"You don't get to lie to me about Concei!" I yelled.

Ethan looked completely mystified. I wasn't sure if it was because he didn't know what I was talking about or because he couldn't figure out how I knew. "Why in the world are you bringing up Concei?"

"Can I have my gas?" I asked, pointing at the nozzle he was still holding.

Ethan shook his head, inserted it in the tank and pushed the appropriate buttons. "You need to tell me why you're bringing up Concei?"

"Because you told me you weren't with her anymore." I rolled my eyes. "I know we're not dating. I know I told you I wouldn't ever date you, but you can't pursue me when you know you're already with her. That's not fair. We've been friends for too long for you to lie to me like that."

Ethan shook his head again. "I have no idea what you're talking about."

"I read an interview someone did with her yesterday. She said you and she were still together."

He frowned. "She wouldn't do that."

"She did and why would she if it wasn't true?"

Ethan shrugged. "I don't know. Let's find out." He rounded his truck and returned with his phone and put it on speaker.

A woman answered. "Hello Sweetheart." Her thick accent sounded sexy and exotic. My heart sank.

"Connie, I need to ask you a question."

"Without asking me how I am?" She sounded more flirty than annoyed.

Ethan rubbed the top of his head with his free hand. "Please, Connie, I need you to answer a question for me."

"Sounds serious. Go on."

"You did an interview recently and said we were dating."

"No," she replied.

Ethan nodded. "Okay, that's what I thought." He moved the phone away from his mouth and eyes widended at me said, "See, I told you."

Then Concei spoke."I did say you were participating in the Heart Foundation Fundraiser with me. You agreed months ago, sweetheart."

Ethan's brow knitted. "I don't remember that."

"You have been my partner for the casino games for the last three years and I win big money for the charity. I mentioned it to you a few months ago you said, sure as long as I don't elope by then," she paused. "You haven't gotten married have you?"

"No, Con." He gave me the side eye. "Look, I have to go. I appreciate you taking the call. I'll explain later."

"It sounds like I need to get a partner. I'll work on that. Chow." She ended the call.

I swallowed a lump of anger that must have gone to my heart because it began to pound wildly. Ethan closed the small space between us. He put his phone on the roof of the car and picked me up. I wrapped my arms around his neck. He pressed my back side against the vehicle and said, "I guess now I get to do this." He covered my lips with his and I let him.

Chapter 12

The next morning Ethan was on a flight to France to attend a memorial in honor of his deceased teammate. I thought it was a good thing, his leaving. He had been such a distraction that I needed him gone, so I could focus on finishing all the details for the wedding. Now that he'd really kissed me, my emotions were on ten.

I was making the place cards for the reception, the favors and the centerpieces for the tables myself. A lot of work, but it was the only way to get it all done at a cost effective price and in time for the wedding.

The three days that he was gone were almost unbearable. I'd never admit that to him or anyone else, but I was seriously getting the shakes from "Ethan Wright" withdrawal symptoms. Without Ethan there was no one giving me incessant compliments, no one to laugh at my sarcastic humor, and no one to spend time with to get away from the evenings with Terrance and Janette. Ethan had been extremely useful.

We video conferenced once a day. He also sent me text messages and emailed me pictures. The pictures were of himself, his friends, and various buildings around Paris. He even made a few videos giving me mini tours. He was so much fun.

My phone rang to the tune of "911" by Wyclef Jean and Mary J. Blige. Ethan had assigned his number to the ringtone the night before he left to ensure I didn't miss any of his calls or text messages in the wave of wedding communication I was getting. I pushed the button to read the text that said, *"FT"* which meant open video conferencing. I obediently and happily pushed the app for

FaceTime on my iPad.

I stared at his handsome face on the screen. We'd already talked for an hour this morning while he traveled to the airport. We'd been interrupted by airport security.

"So, they let you in the terminal," I teased.

"Yes, my bionic knee gets me a full cavity search every time."

"And yet, you keep flying all over the world."

"Can't let a little thing like that keep me down," he said. "Promise me the next time I'm on a flight here that you're with me. You have to visit to really appreciate the beauty."

"If you pay for the plane ticket," I replied, smiling.

"I'm going to hold you to it." He paused for a moment. "I've decided to go to the funeral. I'll have to leave the morning after the wedding to get to South Africa on time."

I nodded. I felt sad, but selfishly not for his friend. I was too focused on my own loss. I'd just had three days without him and now he'd be going even further away. My heart was cracking.

"I wish you had a passport so you could join me. I'd love to show you the country."

I was silent. I fought hard not to let disappointment show on my face. I clasped my hands together and pressed the nervous energy into my palms. "His parents will be glad to see you."

He nodded. "I'm honored to know his family and guess what? I'm playing the piano during the service."

"That's nice," I said forcing excitement into my voice.

He stood. "It's time for me to board."

I could hardly clear the knot in my throat. "Have a good flight."

"I will.". He hesitated for a moment like he wanted to say something else.

Adrenaline shot to my heart. My women's intuition told me I wanted to hear what he had on his mind. "What's up?" I asked, giving him a little nudge.

He scratched the side of his face and shook his head a bit like he was unsure, which wasn't like him. "Nothing. I'll text you when I get on the ground."

I nodded. The moment was lost, but my heart was still pounding.

We ended the call, but it did not stop the tirade of mixed emotions running through me. I felt warm and happy because I'd talked to him; because I'd be seeing him in less than twelve hours. But on the heels of my joy came fear and confusion. In less than forty eight hours he'd be on his way to Africa, the continent that had become like home for him. When was he coming back? Was he coming back? Would he still text and call me? I had no idea what he and I were actually doing. We weren't a couple. All we'd done was kiss and proclaim our unyielding attraction to each other. And if Ethan proposed a thing like "us" trying a relationship I couldn't imagine it working. I wasn't leaving New York,certainly not for a boyfriend, even if he was sexy and smart and rich. Mature women just didn't do that. They didn't pick up and move for men they weren't married to. That was young girl mess.

I sighed and turned my attention back to the mirror. I'd been twisting my hair for the last hour. The creating of my Celie braids didn't seem to phase Ethan one bit. I smiled at the thought. Just one more thing to love about him, he liked my hair.

I did two more plaits and it was finished. All I had to do was untwist it before dinner tonight. I pinned it into a hairstyle that would work when I left the house later to run my last minute errands. I pushed my hair butter aside and pulled the copy of the seating chart in front of me and checked it against the escort cards. It was my third time checking my work. There was no point. I knew it was correct. I was done with everything. I just needed to show up in the morning to supervise the decorating committee, and then I could get dressed and airbrushed like all the other women in the wedding party.

I sighed. This had been an incredibly long week. It was seven thirty a.m. and I'd already been up for hours. I looked at my reflection in the mirror and decided to go back to bed and see if I could snag some much needed beauty rest.

***

It was the ringing of the doorbell that woke me. I reached for my cell phone to check the time. It was nearly noon. I heard the shower going and realized I would have to be the one to get the door, so I popped up and trotted down the stairs. It was a teenage boy. After a moment, I recognized him as Evie's son from the bridal shop with our dress delivery. I pulled the door open, accepted our package and gave him a tip. I did a quick inspection of both, finishing just as Janette stuck her head down over the stair railing. "Is that my dress?" she squealed.

"It is." I hung the bag up over the foyer closet door.

She disappeared from the hallway, but I heard her coming down five minutes later. She unzipped the bag. "Ooo wee! I can't believe it. One more day and I'm going to be Mrs. Terrance Wright."

I swallowed. Hearing that still felt weird.

Janette pushed back the sides of the bag and let the skirt of the dress flow freely. "It's so pretty. I know I just had it on the day before yesterday, but I want to try it on again."

"Can't hurt to make sure it's perfect." I took the bag upstairs and Janette followed me. I helped my sister into her dress and grabbed a few hairpins off the dresser to pin her hair up the way it would be tomorrow.

"My jewelry," she said and threw her hands over her mouth. "Oh, you're going to kill me. My pregnancy brain. I forgot the jeweler called yesterday to say the pieces were ready."

I wasn't going to kill her. It was my job to remember the jeweler and I'd forgotten.

"I'm sorry, Niecy. Do you have time to get them today?"

I glanced at my watch. "No problem. I have to pick up a few things anyway, so let me go now."

"Thank you. You have no idea how much this means to me. What a blessing you've been to me. I know you're my sister, but what you've done." Her eyes filled with tears that began to spill onto her cheeks. Janette reached up and wrapped her arms around my neck. I gave her a long hug. As trying as this week had been, it was impossible for me to be angry with her for long. I loved her too much. She and I were all we had and the truth was she'd always been spoiled, selfish and competitive with me about everything. She hadn't changed a bit.

I pulled some facial tissues from the box and dabbed at her eyes. "We can't have a mascara stain on this dress, so let's get you out of it."

I helped her take off the dress and returned it to the hanger. Then I grabbed my handbag and exited the house. Ethan had left me his truck. At first, I didn't think it was necessary. Once I drove it a few times, I found I enjoyed the size. It made me feel closer to him and reminded me of his not so amateur counseling session that helped me deal with the nausea. It also smelled like him. That was the best perk of them all.

I drove into downtown Garrison. My first stop was for Janette's jewelry. I inspected the items and left the shop with them in a crush proof box. Next, I stopped by the bakery to decorate the cake. I'd chosen to add flowers around the perimeter of each layer. These were the only artificial flowers in the entire wedding. I'd had to custom order pink Heather from a florist in New York, because the local florist wasn't sure he would have them in time. Flowers were a big deal. I made sure to find the best quality for my brides.

I stepped back and surveyed the cake. It was perfect and it'd be perfect tomorrow, because of course, artificial flowers didn't wilt. It was a simple, yet effective way to pull the cake into the theme. I confirmed the delivery time with the owner and was on my way.

My phone rang as I was getting back in the truck. It was Terrance. I sent the call to voicemail. It rang again. I sent it to voicemail a second time. Then I received a text that simply said: *We should talk.*

I sighed. I was out of time on running from him. He and Janette were getting married tomorrow and it was obvious he had something he wanted to say to me. I had to get this conversation over, because tomorrow he would be family. I couldn't be in this place at Thanksgiving and Christmas. I had nephew to visit. He and I had to work it out. I pushed the button to make the call.

"I was starting to think you'd never talk to me," he said.

I sighed. "What do you want Terrance?"

"Ten minutes of your time."

"I'm on the phone. You have it."

"Not like this. I need to see you." I knew from his tone, he wouldn't back down on our meeting being face to face, but I still attempted to do it my way.

"Why can't we talk on the phone?"

"Because I want to avoid a misunderstanding," he replied. "Let's meet at the old Chambers complex on Highway 54. I'm renting some space there."

I knew the area. There used to be a general store and a slew of other stores at that location, but Wal-mart came to town and put the little guys out of business.

"I need to come now. I have a lot to do –"

He cut me off. "Now is perfect. I'm on my way there."

I sent a text to Gayle.

Me: *Going to meet with Terrance to have the talk.*

Gayle: *In the nick of time I'd say.*

Me: *Pray it goes well.*

Gayle: *Speak from your heart, not your emotions. Praying.*

I turned off Main Street and began to creep along the back road that led to the location I assumed was Terrance's site for his new business. I was dreading this conversation, but Terrance was right, we needed to say whatever needed to be said before he and my sister became husband and wife.

It wasn't that I thought our conversation would stop a wedding. I didn't love Terrance and I was sure he didn't love me, but I was in my feelings. He knew it and he knew why, so this conversation needed to happen.

I made a right onto the street I was looking for and spotted his truck outside in the parking lot. It was the only vehicle there. I parked and he met me at the door.

The space was huge. They'd knocked down the walls

connecting the stores and made one large open facility. It extended back for what I reasoned to be half the length of a New York City block.

I crossed my arms over my chest. The clicking of my steel stiletto heels filled the cavernous space until I stopped at Terrance's desk. "Ethan didn't tell me what you were planning to do here. He's a silent partner in more ways than one."

Terrance exhaled a long breath. He seemed to be relieved. I wondered if he thought I was going to come in here screaming and hollering.

"I asked him not to tell anyone. I wanted to get all the money lined up."

"And surprise Janette with the Investment Bank episode?" I asked raising an eyebrow. "Ethan did tell me about that."

He smiled and tapped his fist against his palm. "Money is bound to pour in after the show. People invest whether the bankers on the show do or not."

"So what's the plan? What's the business?"

"Building furniture for pop-up houses."

I gave him the explain look.

"A pop-up is a kind of pre-fab home. The company we're in business with is making the houses out of shipping containers."

I'd seen news stories about this before, but I hadn't really paid close attention, so I asked, "Are pop-up houses supposed to be the new trailer home?"

"No," he said, "Well, yes, they could be, but we're focusing on third world countries where there are housing shortages like South Africa."

"I thought people were doing that already."

"They are but not near enough. The market for this is wide open and our furniture model is a little more innovative. Let me show you the plans."

I followed him inside where he showed me plans and sketches and videos of what they were doing. It was cool stuff. I was impressed.

"How in the world did you become interested in something like this?"

"It was Ethan. The stories he'd tell when he came home. The documentary he did for CNN a few years ago really tugged at my heart. I just knew there had to be something we could do here."

"And it creates jobs," I said uncrossing my arms.

"The plant isn't going to make it. I'm on the inside track enough to know that."

"This is interesting. It's great that you and Ethan are working together. It must be nice to know he's got your back."

"Kind of like you have Janette's with this wedding," he said. His subtle lead in was right on time. We needed to get to the point of this meeting. "I really appreciate you doing everything you've done for us. I know it's not just been about the planning. I know money is involved too."

I gave him the explanation I'd given everyone else who marveled at my effort. "She's my sister."

"I know that, but still…"

"I'm loyal like that. Unlike some other people I know."

"So, are you saying it was disloyal of me to fall in love with her?"

"It was disloyal to me and to God, not to mention your father's ministry and my father's memory for you to get her pregnant."

Terrance nodded. "That may be true, but I'm human, Nec...Deniece. It's not the first time I've been disloyal to you and God, my father's ministry and your father's memory as you so painstakingly put it."

We both knew what he was talking about. The night I lost the virginity I'd held onto for thirty years. I shook my head. "I don't know what to feel Terrance. I'm thirty-five and I keep wondering if I missed my chance at a husband and kids because I wouldn't stay in Garrison and marry my childhood sweetheart. I'm successful career-wise, but there are some days when I wish I'd just kept it simple," I cried. "But when I feel like that I feel badly, especially now that Janette is pregnant and she's excited about getting married. I just don't know how to let go of you being for me and not her. Do you understand what I'm saying?"

"But you don't love me," Terrance stated, firmly.

"No," I shook my head like the fact that I didn't love him hadn't really entered into the equation. "I don't, but –"

He raised a hand. "You wanted me to be the guy in the glass case that you could come back to, if you were desperate and decided home was good enough for you."

"I never snubbed home. I just always dreamed of living in New York."

Terrance stuck his hands in trousers. "Well, your dream came true."

I held my tongue. There was no point in letting the words on my mind come out of my mouth, because they were mean. I was trying not to speak out of my 'bitter' emotions. "How do I become your sister-in-law after we've been lovers?"

Terrance sighed heavily. "It was just that one time."

"My first time."

"I know and I'm sorry I took something so special. But if our family is going to move forward, if the future is going to work, you have to try to put what you and I had in past."

I squeezed my arms around my chest. "Have you?"

He nodded. "I have. I didn't have a choice."

"So, it's a like a switch you turn off?"

"It's something I've prayed off."

I twisted my lips in doubt. "You sure about that? You've been really foul with Ethan this week. You actually hit him."

Terrance was silent and then said, "I was trying to protect you. Ethan is young and he's been kind of unsettled. You don't need that."

I bit my tongue and started a count to ten in my head. How dare he think he had the right to decide who or what I needed.

I'd only gotten to three when he said, "Nectar, I –

"Don't call me that!" I yelled. "It stopped being a childhood nickname when you whispered it in my ear when you were making love to me."

Terrance's frustration rose. He dropped into the chair behind his desk. "Deniece, you can't keep doing this. I love Janette. And if I'm honest with myself, I'll admit she reminds me of you."

"This is getting weirder." I shook my head. "You know that Janette and I are nothing alike."

"You're more alike than you know."

I crossed my arms over my chest again and cocked my head forward. He couldn't mean what I was interpreting it to be. "You're not telling me you're marrying my sister because she reminds you of me. I may not be happy with this situation, but I love my sister. I don't want her being used."

"You don't have to worry about that. It's not about your personalities." He rose from the chair. "It's your values, the way you love God and care for other people. Your dedication to family. Do you know how hard that is to find these days? People are different. Women have changed."

I dropped my arms.

"She's the Malcolm sister that's right for me and that's why you said no, Deniece. God didn't mean you for me. He meant me to be with Janette."

I bit my bottom lip and shook my head. "So, now God's in the mix?"

Terrance took a few steps toward me. "God has always been in the mix and you know that."

"I need to be sure she won't be hurt. I know you always try to do the right thing."

"My father's a pastor, but it's not the fifties. A man doesn't have to marry a woman just because she's pregnant."

I sighed and tried to process that statement with respect to Terrance's 'do right' ways. "I hear you, but you do remember the circumstances under which you proposed to me?"

A floor board creaked behind us. We simultaneously followed the sound. Janette entered the room. Terrance and I looked at each other and then back at Janette. With our eyes, we asked the same question. How long had she been standing there? Had she heard everything that we'd said?

Terrance rushed to her side. "Janie, baby, you shouldn't be out like this." He was crooning in a tone I'd never heard him use before. It was a bit over the top. That was making us look guilty. "And you know the doctor specifically said you shouldn't drive."

"I know what the doctor said," Janette snapped and

snatched her arm out of his grasp. "I tried to call you and ask you to bring me some ice cream. Then I decided I should get out for a bit, so I drove myself. I drove by on the chance you were here and imagine my surprise to see Ethan's truck."

"We were talking about the wedding," I interjected, lying poorly.

Janette cocked her head. "Something you couldn't say over the phone."

"Ethan is on his way from the airport. I was going to see him, so I thought I'd ride by on the way."

She rolled her eyes. "On the way. I'd say this is a bit out of the way to Ethan's place."

"Honey, that still doesn't excuse you disobeying doctor's orders. You go on home and I'll follow and double back to Dolan's and get your ice cream."

"Don't mess with my head, Terrance. I walked in on a heated discussion. You and my sister seem to have some things to say to each other. Please continue where you left off. You know the part about the marriage proposal." Janette's eyes were wet with tears. "Why didn't you tell me you proposed to my sister?"

Terrance looked terrified. "I didn't think it was important," he stuttered. He looked to me. I turned my head. He was going to have to work this out alone.

"I always thought the relationship between you and Niecy had been more friends than a real couple. I thought you were pals who hung out together."

I crossed my arms in front of my chest, raised an eyebrow at my sister. "Pals that hung out?" My tone challenged her. It was time for the denial to stop.

Janette pursed her lips against the lie. "Okay, I knew you

were a couple, but I didn't know you were serious about her or that she had been serious about you. Not proposal serious." She deliberately turned her back to me and faced Terrance.

Terrance shook his head. "What difference does it make now? That was a long time ago."

"Not that long and don't tell me it doesn't matter because the two of you are here talking about it." We were silent. She continued. "Now I understand why everyone has been looking at me strange and why my own sister has seemed so different this week. I guess I was somewhere with my head in the clouds, being excited about finally finding the man of my dreams and building a future that I didn't consider how our relationship would look to everyone."

The man of her dreams. Those words struck me. I cast a glance in Terrance's direction. I'd never thought of him that way. Was that what my sister really felt when she looked at him? I supposed it was possible.

Suddenly, I was struck. I remembered why I was here. I was taking care of my sister, fulfilling my promise to my father. I dropped my arms and cleared my throat. "Don't worry about everyone else. This is your life. The proposal is long behind us."

"Right, and I didn't really mean it when I asked," he added.

I rolled my neck on that comment. He quickly tried to clean it up. "I mean. I'd done something and it seemed like the right thing to do at the time."

"You'd done something." Frustrated, Janette tunneled her fingers through her bone straight tresses. "What had you done that made you feel like you needed to propose, because in my case you got me pregnant?"

Terrance swallowed hard. He'd said too much. "This

stress isn't good for the baby."

"A bad marriage won't be good for it either," she snapped.

I interjected. "I said no. It's like you said before, I broke up with him, twice, so what does it matter about why?"

"I know I'm not the sharpest knife in the drawer but I walked in on a discussion about your ex-engagement, so don't tell me it doesn't matter."

"Daddy had just died and he thought it would be a comfort to me if he asked me. In fact, he asked me the next day."

"You were gone all night the night the of daddy's funeral. I remember that. Were you with him?" She turned to Terrance. "Did you have sex with my sister?"

"Janette, baby—"

"It's a simple yes or no question, Terrance. Did you?"

He hung his head. "Yes."

Janette whipped her body around to face me. "God, Niecy. Why didn't you tell me that?"

I shrugged. "You didn't tell me you were dating him and what would have been the point? You were already pregnant."

"You should have told me, both of you." Janette began to move backward out of the room. Tears were streaming down her face. She released a shuddering sob. "I can't. I'm not going to be able to do this. The wedding is off." She turned and left the room.

"Janette, wait!" Terrance followed her. I could hear his pleas and then the sound of her car ripping down the gravel road. I closed my eyes. I shouldn't have come here. I should have just let sleeping dogs lie.

Chapter 13

I was as nervous as a stripper in church. Janette hadn't returned to the house. We'd already gone through the rehearsal for the ceremony with one of the hostesses standing in for Janette. That was easy to explain. She was on bed rest and the bride's role in the wedding was relatively simple; to walk down the aisle on cue. I joked and said, "My sister has been watching videos of women walking down the aisle for weeks. Don't worry, she knows exactly how to make her entrance." A few people laughed and we finished the rehearsal without incident.

Now it was time for us to head down to the fellowship hall where the church's women's ministry was hosting the dinner. A bead of sweat trickled down my back. I looked at my watch. It was nearly eight o'clock. I couldn't believe she wasn't going to show up for all this.

I glanced at Terrance. He was standing near the window looking like he'd throw up at any moment. One of his groomsman joked, "Well T, if she's not showing up for the rehearsal, she's probably skipping the real thing."

A few people laughed. I was tempted to take out my cell phone and pretend to have a conversation with Janette expressing regrets, but like Ethan had just told me, "*This is Terrance's problem. Let him sweat it out*".

I looked in Ethan's eyes and he squeezed my hand. I was so glad he was back. I'd missed him like crazy and unless I was delusional, he seemed awfully glad to see me as well. "It's not just Terrance's problem. She's my sister. She's hurting."

Ethan raised a hand to stroke my face. "Janette loves him. They'll work it out." He scooted his chair a little closer to me. "Have I told you how amazing you look?"

I blushed. "No, but it's never too late for that."

"Your hair turned out great." He released my hand, sat back and gave me a brazen once over from my head to my stilettos. "Everything looks great."

I was about to be generous with a compliment of my own, when out of my peripheral vision, I saw Terrance bolt from the window like he was on fire. I looked out and Janette's car came into sight.

"Thank God," I whispered under my breath.

"Told you," Ethan replied.

I stood and shot out of the room and into the main hallway behind Terrance.

"Baby, I've been so worried," I heard him say. "Where have you been?"

Janette raised a hand to stop him from embracing her. "I'm here to tell my family and friends that the wedding is cancelled. Telling them in person is the proper thing to do."

"Honey, please," Terrance pleaded. "Don't do this. Let's talk."

"There's nothing you can say." Janette was emphatic. Her puffy eyes told the story, she'd been crying for hours. My heart sank. I stepped forward.

"What about me?" I began.

Janette shook her head. "Niecy, this is between me and my fiancé. I'd prefer it stayed that way."

"Well, I'm going to have to play the big sister card here." I took her hand and pulled her into a nearby office. "I came all the way from New York to plan and execute your wedding. I've spent thousands of dollars." I could tell Janette was going to interrupt me so I stopped her with my index finger. "I promised daddy on his dying bed that I would take care of you. That I'd make sure you were okay, so I think all of that entitles me to have my say."

Janette put a hand on her hip and reluctantly rolled her eyes in my direction. "Daddy told you to take care of me?"

I nodded. "He did, but I haven't had to. You've done a great job of doing it all by yourself."

My sister let out a long breath. "What great job? I mess everything up. I never finished college. I work in hair salon as a receptionist and shampoo girl because I never finished my beauty school training. I'm six months pregnant by a man who doesn't love me. You tell me how I've done a great job?"

"Don't do that. Don't decide that because you don't have a fancy career you haven't accomplished anything." I took a few steps toward her. "Janette, people love you. You're kind to everyone and you have so many friends. Sometimes the greatest success we can have in life is through relationships."

"But the one that means the most to me has been a lie. How can I marry a man who proposed to you? He loved you first. He wanted you first." She paused and this time her eye roll was intended to cut. "He had you first."

"Janette, Terrance and I were intimate, but I initiated it. I was sad about daddy. I'd broken up with another guy in New York prior to coming home, so I was on the rebound. Terrance was there for me before and after the funeral. I was feeling lonely and rejected. Once it was over, he realized that it was my first time and I could tell he felt bad about that. The next night he came over and he asked me to marry him. He was talking about the Bible and how a man that takes a woman's virginity is like a thief and all that stuff he's had mixed up in his head."

"He's right about some of that," Janette said.

I shrugged. "That's debatable, but one thing we know for sure is that he's honorable. But no matter how honorable he was and how much I cared about him, I knew I had no intentions of staying in Garrison. I also knew Terrance would never leave. That meant we could never be together, virginity gone or not, so I said no to his proposal. You should have seen the relief on his face."

"But, he did love you."

"Maybe, in high school or college, but it doesn't matter, because he doesn't love me today."

"How do I know he's not marrying me for the same reason he asked you? Obligation. I don't want him marrying me because I'm pregnant. I love Terrance. I want him to feel the same way about me. How do I know?"

"That's easy," Terrance said, entering the room.

I stepped aside and let him take my place in front of Janette. He took her hand. "You look into my eyes when I tell you and you know because you trust me."

Janette pulled her hand from his and looked away. "I don't trust you. Not anymore."

"You trusted me six hours ago. I haven't changed." He sat down and pulled her onto his lap. "You have to believe me when I tell you this. I fell in love with you six months ago. You smiled at me from across the room and I swear my heart burst open."

Her gaze met his and her expression softened. "That night was so romantic."

Terrance pulled her hand to his heart. "I really saw you for the first time."

"And I saw you." Janette's voice cracked and her eyes wet with new tears. "It felt like something from a romance novel. Love at first sight."

Terrence had this. I cleared my throat. "I'm going to give you two the room." They were in each other's arms crying and kissing and apologizing before I made it through the door.

I stepped out and bumped into Ethan.

"So, are they jumping the broom or what?"

"They are," I replied. "I think this blow out, as stressful as it was, needed to happen. No one is going into the marriage wondering if it was the right thing to do."

Ethan nodded. "It's important to know someone loves you for who you are without a bunch of other stuff in the way."

I didn't respond to that.

He took my hand and pulled it to his mouth. The heat of his lips and gaze caused me to melt. "It's getting late. I need to get Janette and Terrance in there." I gently pulled my hand from his grasp.

Ethan nodded. "I'll let you do your job." He turned and walked into the fellowship hall. I let my body go limp against the wall. How in the world had I come home, angry with one Wright and fallen so hard for another?

Chapter 14

The wedding of Terrance Wright to Janette Malcolm would be the talk of the town in Garrison for a long time. Janette was a beautiful bride. Her deep cocoa skin glowed like shimmery chestnuts against the backdrop of her white dress and veil. A last minute change during styling, she'd opted to wear her hair down rather than up as planned. It cascaded around her face in a pool of spiral curls. Her headpiece, a tiara fashioned from crystal and three layers of an exquisite shimmery voile fabric, sat on the crown of her head and hung down her back. The dress itself was stunning and although Janette walked proudly down the aisle, it did a good job of concealing her pregnancy so she didn't look like a Weeble Wobble who should have been rolled. It also swept the floor. No one knew that underneath she wore modest two-inch heels I'd suggested for comfort. The final touch was the bouquet, a festive assortment of white flowers tied with a sprig of fuchsia heather. She looked perfect.

Terrance was equally as handsome in his black and gray tuxedo with fuchsia accessories. I'd never seen him look more handsome or happy. They made a fine couple. I thought my parents would be proud.

Reverent Wright did a traditional Christian ceremony. My eyes had been misty throughout the entire thing, but when he did the pronouncement, I was overcome with emotion.

"Because Terrance and Janette have desired each other in marriage, and have witnessed this before God and our gathering, affirming their acceptance of the responsibilities of such a union, and have pledged their love and faith to each other, sealing their vows in the giving and receiving of rings, I do proclaim that they are husband and wife in the sight of God and man. Let all people here and everywhere recognize and respect this holy union, now and forever. Amen."

Everyone in the sanctuary stood. A tear fell with the revelation I was one of the people who had to respect this union, now and forever. This marriage was not about two people's past. It was about the future of two people that I loved who loved each other.

I looked up and whispered, "I hear you God. Loud and clear."

Reverend Wright said a closing prayer and they kissed. "It is now my privilege to introduce to you for the first time, my son and daughter-in-law, Mr. and Mrs. Terrence Braxton Wright."

***

The reception line was finished and the D.J. hadn't arrived. I stepped out of the room while the photographer took shots of the groomsmen and called him. His car wouldn't start. His brother-in-law had just arrived and they were piling into his car and on the way to the hall. Unfortunately, they were still twenty minutes away. I encouraged him to drive safely and returned to the reception.

What was I going to do? I had a CD with music on it as a back up, but the equipment wasn't working. I'd tested it last night and it was fine. Today, it was like it'd been struck by lightening and died.

Ms. Marie, the wedding coordinator approached me. "The music?"

"Twenty minutes away," I replied.

"But it's time for the first dance."

I gave her a look. Like I didn't know that. "We'll have to change the order of the events. We can have them cut the cake first." I stopped mid-sentence, because I caught sight of my salvation. A small child, no more than five was being pulled away from a piano by a woman who looked like an exhausted mother. I scanned the room, zoomed in on Ethan as he laughed with the groomsmen and excused myself.

I interrupted Ethan's conversation with a polite, "I need to borrow you for a second."

He followed me. "What's up?"

"The piano. Have you ever played in front of anyone other than your music teacher or some woman you were trying to impress?"

"A few times. Mostly impromptu church stuff," he replied. "Why?"

"My D.J.'s running late. I'd really like to keep the schedule we have because it flows right, but I need Terrance and Janette to have their first dance."

He raised an eyebrow. "You want me to play in front of all these people?"

"Would you?" I asked.

He looked at the guest, glanced at the piano and then back at me.

I mouthed the word, *please.*

His eyes stayed on my lips a little longer than they should have. He cleared his throat. "Sure. I'm going to have to play at the funeral in few days, so why not. This'll be good practice for me."

"Great!" I clapped my hands and hugged him. "You're the best."

"You don't know the half of it." He smiled. "What's their song?"

"The Closer I Get to You."

"Hmm, that's two people, one being a woman, so I can't pull that off, but I do know some Luther."

"At this point anything will do."

He walked over to the piano, played with his phone for a few seconds and within minutes he made the piano hum. Ethan was such a ham that he took over Ms. Marie's job of announcing the couple. He shared a childhood story about him and Terrance, which caused laughter to fill the hall. Then he shared a story about some humorous incident at church with Janette, after which he led into the music from "So Amazing" by Luther Vandross. He was no Luther, but dang, the brother could blow. When he wasn't checking his phone for what I presumed had to be the music, he was looking at me. A few people followed his eyes to me and I couldn't help but blush, which I could tell he loved. I turned away for a few moments. This man was so bold it was downright ratchet. I wasn't used to someone with such a strong personality and I wondered if dating men who were more subdued was another way my control issues manifested. Ethan made me feel like I was on some type of rollercoaster ride, like that feeling I used to get when my stomach dropped in a car or on a plane. I texted Gayle.

Me: *He's playing and singing So Amazing by Luther.*

Gayle: *Amazing.*

Me: *He makes me feel like I don't have control. I don't like it.*

Gayle: *I understand, but you'll never know love until you let go and surrender to it. Stop being afraid and give that beggin' man a chance before I kill you!*

I giggled inwardly. That was not the response that would

help me maintain my resolve and I realized that's why I texted Gayle. She was the friend who would encourage me to step out of my comfort zone. I turned around and instead of finding Ethan's eyes I focused on Janette and Terrance. They were touched by Ethan's playing. My sister's eyes were brimming with unshed tears. She and her new husband glided across the floor instep to Ethan's singing and the guests were just as moved by their dancing as they were by Ethan's playing. Reverend and Mother Wright never picked their jaws up off the floor the entire time he played. He apparently hadn't shared his new found talent with them either.

Just as he finished, the D.J. entered the room and set up to take over. The audience gave Janette, Terrance and Ethan a standing ovation. "The Closer I Get to You" piped through the speakers and the floor filled with couples.

Chapter 15

The reception was almost over. The guests were eating cake, gathering favors and taking advantage of their last opportunity to chat with the wedding party.

I was making my rounds giving the tip envelopes to the people who served us and the vendors who hadn't yet received theirs. I'd just come in from talking to the limo driver when I heard Ethan's laugh come from a room away from the general crowd. I intended to join him, but before I could step in I heard Terrance speak.

"I didn't mean to be so hard on you. I just had to see where you were coming from. Deniece is a special woman."

"You're lucky I let you get away with the black eye."

Terrance chuckled. "I owed you that from that basketball game last year. You know you threw that elbow on purpose."

They both laughed. I smiled. It was nice to hear them laughing together.

"Anyway, you know Deniece was my first love. I'm always going to care about her."

"I hear you, but I have to admit I was kind of concerned about where your head was." I heard Ethan say.

"I didn't want her hurt. I didn't want you to use her and discard her when she was vulnerable."

"Like you did five years ago?"

"I admit, I should have handled some things better," Terrance replied. "But it doesn't matter now, because you are the right Wright for her."

There was a break in their conversation and then Ethan spoke. "I don't know. I can't tell. She keeps running from me."

Terrance chuckled. "Nectar's hard to catch. Take it from the man who never caught her, but you should love that about her. It confirms you two are alike. You have big dreams. You both know how to go for it. She needs someone like that."

Ethan was silent. Terrance continued. "I was attracted to her spirit, but I wasn't going to sprout wings and fly away with it. I also would have never let her fly."

There was a beat of silence. I strained to try to hear what they were saying.

"I love you like a little brother, so I'm warning you, don't mess this up," Terrance said.

"I'm trying not to," Ethan replied, "but I don't know. I'm not even sure if she really wants me."

Do I want him? I asked myself as I escaped down the hall. I needed privacy, but there was no privacy to be found in this place. The ladies room, living room and the waiting area were full. As I moved from space to space discovering this, people who complimented me on the beautiful decorations and the splendor of the event stopped me. I had requests for my business cards. People had events in their future that they wanted me to plan for them. I handed out cards but I couldn't digest any of it, because I had to get my head together. The only place I could find was a broom closet. I slipped inside and turned on the dim light.

Do I want him? "God help me, I do, but I'm scared. He's so perfect. There's got to be something wrong with him."

I spotted a stool in the corner of the room. I reasoned it was clean enough and sat. Five minutes and I'd be back out there lending a hand to Sister Marie and the hostesses;

ensuring the top layer of Janette's cake was properly packed and the cards were secured to every wedding present, lest they get separated in travel. Then I'd assist the hostesses in getting a sparkler into the hand of every guest. The finale had the guest lined up between the front steps and the limo framing Terrance and Janette's exit with a lighted arch. It was spectacular every time I did it. Janette would love it. I had to get out there to do those things. I just needed a minute to stop the tremors in my soul.

I felt nauseous just like I had behind the wheel of a car and on a plane all these years. Just like my car and plane nausea, I was afraid now because I wouldn't have control. Ethan had helped me with that. Helped me to remember through my faith I had no fear, but now the very person who had encouraged me to not be afraid had me terrified. I didn't even know what to do with so much man. Fine as Michael Ealy, rich, well traveled, smart, spiritual, and …fine. Way too fine to be corralled by anyone, forget someone like me. No matter how much time I spent in New York City and no matter how high I stood on my designer heels, I was still just a country girl; a country mouse in the big city. I wasn't sure I had enough of what he needed. I couldn't bare it if I fell any deeper in love and he dumped me. I squeezed my eyes shut. Just the thought of that kind of heartbreak…

"Has anyone seen Deniece?" I heard Ethan's voice outside the room. I stood and stepped closer to the door. Someone asked if he'd checked the ladies room and he responded, "I had one of the bridesmaids check in there. I've looked everywhere." He mumbled something I couldn't hear and then "Someone Please Call 911" rang out from my cell phone.

"Did you hear that?" Ethan asked. "Where did that come from?"

I reached into my skirt for the phone and it rang louder. I'd forgotten I turned the volume up when I was waiting to hear from the D.J.

There was a light rap on the door and then Ethan's voice. "Deniece?"

The door opened. Ethan blocked the light that flooded the small room. I could see the group he had been talking to standing behind him. He made a half turn towards them and said, "I found her. Apparently she does floors too." They laughed. He stepped in the room and closed the door.

"What are you doing?" I asked.

"Joining you. Why are you in here? You couldn't be planning to mop."

I rolled my eyes. "I'm getting a moment to myself, so would you please go back out."

"By myself?"

"Yes."

Ethan chuckled. "No way, baby. People are not going to say I came out of the closet at Terrance's wedding."

I got the joke.

He continued, "Word will be all over Garrison before they got the communion crackers out. Chile, Ethan came out at the wedding." He laughed. "No ma'am. Either we go out together or we stay in here together."

I shook my head. "You're so silly." I wanted to say, *I love that about you,* but I stopped myself. "So, now that we've established I'm not leaving, tell me, why do you need a moment to yourself?"

"I'm thinking?"

"About?" he asked and then he seemed to realize something. A slight smile touched his strong mouth as he crossed his arms over his crisp white shirt. "Are you thinking about me?"

"Why would you assume that?"

"I don't know. I'm confident."

I smirked. "Overconfident."

"Yesterday you said I was making you crazy. You're in a broom closet at your sister's wedding. That's pretty crazy behavior."

I shook my head. "I should go. I have work to do."

Ethan stepped back. He wasn't letting me pass. "No, we talk, now, because you're making us both crazy." He reached for my arm and pulled me to him. I collided with his chest like I was bumping into a brick wall. I liked that feeling, a lot. "I love you," he said.

Shock paralyzed me for a moment.He had not even hesitated. I shook my head. "Love me?"

"Everything about you." He dropped a kiss on the top of my head.

I melted. "Things have been moving so fast. How can you be so sure?"

He used a finger to lift my chin so my eyes met his. "Remember, I told you, men always know."

My heart knocked against my chest. I took a deep breath. I wanted to step back, but there was no place to go. There was nowhere to run in this tiny space.

"I know it seems like it's only been twelve days, but it hasn't. I've loved you since you had pigtails."

Smiling, I rested my head against his chest. His heart was pounding just as wildly as mine. I wasn't the only one who was scared. Why did I think that I was?

"And you," he continued, raising my chin again. "You love me too." He swept a finger across my lips. "You don't have to say it right now if you don't want to. I can tell."

I nodded. I did have to say it. I owed him that, because even though he'd given me an out, his spirit was begging me to speak my truth. "I do love you." I released the breath I'd been holding. "I can't imagine going back to my life without you in it."

The corners of his lips went up. Satisfied he said, "Then don't be scared. Do what you did when you picked up and moved to New York. Take a risk."

"I, I can't," I cried, moving out of his grasp. "I don't know how to be with someone who spends most of his time overseas. I'm not that secure."

"That doesn't have to be my life anymore. I already told you that. As a matter of fact, the first kid's fitness center is going to be in New York."

I avoided his eyes by locking my gaze at the center of his chest. "When did you decide that?"

He moved a tendril of hair from my face and raised my chin so our eyes met again. "That first night I found you crying on the side of the road."

The air left my lungs. I barely recognized my own voice. "You can't mean that."

His eyes confirmed his words. "I do."

"Ethan."

"We've established that we're two people in love, so I'm not letting you out of this closet until you agree to be my woman."

He squeezed my hands. Time was frozen as we stood there facing each other, our hands clasped; him willing me to say yes and me fighting to say no.

"It's warm in here," Ethan said. "I'm going to have to strip and if someone opens the door and I'm missing clothes..."

I chuckled. "It won't be as bad as it would be if you came out of the closet."

He leaned down and kissed me; nearly lifted me off my feet when he pulled his lips away.

I heard Ribbon in the Sky pipe through the speakers in the background.

"They're playing our song," he whispered.

I smiled and tried to look away. He wouldn't let me. He began to sing. "Oh so long for this night I prayed." I met his eyes. He took my free hand and put it on his shoulder. He led as our bodies moved together. I let my head rest on his shoulder. I pushed out all the negative thoughts in my mind about his age, my age, his wanderlust spirit, the fact that he was practically my exes' brother. I pushed them all aside, pulled my head back to catch his eyes and said, "You told me you make a good boyfriend. I'm holding you to that."

Ethan yelled and picked me up in the air.

"That's the Deniece Malcolm I know." He brought me down low enough for my lips to land on his.

The door to the closet opened. I heard voices, but I didn't care. I was breaking another one of my rules; kissing in public.

"Open your mouth," I whispered. Ethan chuckled and then took great pleasure in complying.

Epilogue

Six months later ...

The long black limousine came to a stop. He stepped out and held his hand for me. I exited in a strapless silk tulle fairytale ball gown with a crystal encrusted bodice. It was the dress I'd dreamed of wearing every time I planned a wedding for another bride. My groom had to be the most handsome man on the planet. The moonlight danced off his vest and the metallic thread shimmered against his thick, tight abs. Lord have mercy, he was all mine.

We walked into the ballroom under the announcement. "Ladies and Gentlemen, I present to you Mr. and Mrs. Ethan Augustus Wright. Our guest applauded. Ethan squeezed my hand and raised it to his lips. We joined the bridal party and greeted our guests as they came through the reception line. There were friends and family from Garrison, Atlanta, New York City and even France, Spain and Africa. It was a highly televised event that ex-pro soccer player, humanitarian and successful businessman, Ethan Wright was getting married in Atlanta this weekend to what was said to be an ex-girlfriend from high school. Cameras from every major entertainment, sports magazine and newspaper flashed.

We completed the reception line and a band began to play. Early in our planning, Ethan had been assigned the task of taking care of the music for the reception. He assured me that every song would be a sweet surprise for me. Four vocalists stepped on the stage and our coordinator announced, "And now, we will have the Wright's first dance."

The women began to sing: *Here we are together. In a place, in a space surrounded by love.*

My heart filled up so much that I closed my eyes to suppress the tears of joy that wanted to flow. How did he know? How could he know that of all the wedding songs I'd heard in my life that this was my very favorite? I opened my eyes and took a step towards my groom. He pulled me into his arms and our guests gushed "Oohs and aahs."

Ethan sang with the women, "You make me so happy. Happy forever." Their voices faded into the background and we danced. "You like?" he asked.

I nodded. "I can't believe you picked that song. How did you know?"

"I know you, baby. You best believe that." He smiled and pulled me closer.

I smiled with him. "I should have known you'd be unpredictable, but you couldn't have told me that we wouldn't be dancing to Ribbon in the Sky."

"I thought I'd save that one for later tonight. I'm planning to sing it until the sun comes up." His dark eyes became devilishly darker.

A rush of heat swept over me. I twisted my lips into a smile and repeated his words. "Until the sun comes up."

"I never did tell you my number one favorite thing to do." He smiled and kissed my chin.

I could hardly wait for the reception to end. I was probably more excited about the honeymoon than he was, but since we were here, I enjoyed it.

When the dance was over, Janette and Terrance joined us on the floor. With tears in her eyes Janette said, "Sis, this is the most beautiful wedding you never planned."

We laughed. "I know. I'm going to have to take lessons from my own wedding planner."

Both our men spun us around and we changed partners. As Janette took Ethan's hand she whispered over her shoulder. "By the way, I just found out I'm pregnant again."

I frowned and stopped moving. "Already? I thought you had to wait a certain amount of time in between pregnancies."

Janette shrugged. Ethan guided her back into Terrance's arms and took my hand. He pulled me into motion and said, "Now, come on, babe, everybody knows the Malcolm sisters don't follow the rules."

I laughed and closed his teasing lips with a kiss.

The End

Reading Group Questions

- Do you think it's acceptable to date a friend or relative's ex? Why or why not?

- If you were in Deniece's place, would you have done so much for Janette? Why or why not?

- Deniece seemed to have quite a few dating rules that may have interfered with her ability to find love. Do you think Deniece's hesitation about Ethan was about those rules or something else?

- Ethan shares that he was angry with Pastor Wright because he wouldn't let his mother live in their father's home without her following his rules. What are your thoughts about how Pastor Wright handled the situation?

- Do you have any dating rules? What are they? Have you ever broken a dating rule? What was the result?

- Weddings can be lavish events. What are your thoughts about people having million dollar weddings and parties in a time when so many people lack the basics of food, clothing and shelter all over the world?

- Discuss wedding songs. What are your favorites?

Excerpt from *Give A Little Love*

By Rhonda McKnight

Chapter 1

"Jesus is the reason for the season." The radio D.J. from Love 101 FM's smooth voice crooned from the stereo speakers on the table next to her. Brooke Jordan flipped the power button to off before he could say another word. Even though Jesus was the reason for the season, her Christmas was going to be *stank* with a capital S. There was no getting around that fact.

Brooke pushed the plantation shutters on the windows open to let in the sounds of the reggae influenced Christmas music rising up from below. She couldn't believe she was spending Christmas week in Montego Bay, Jamaica. It would have been perfect if she wanted to be here, but she didn't. She wasn't on vacation. This wasn't a pleasure trip.
Brooke had drawn the short straw in a staff meeting, so she was stuck working. *Stank,* she thought, *stank on steroids.*

She leaned against the sill of the window, closed her eyes and inhaled a long, intoxicating breath of ocean air. Every aspect of the island was paradise: the weather, the ocean views and the food. There was no doubt about it. But no place was really paradise when you wanted to be somewhere else. Brooke opened her eyes and squinted to see a couple further down the beach. They lay in the sand, making out or maybe even making love. Honeymooners, she knew. She'd seen them arrive a few days ago. Brooke watched as they arrived and others left. She remembered how it was for her when she had honeymooned on an island. She'd been in love like that. She had made love on the beach and then less than two years later, she was signing divorce papers. She tried not to hold it against the entire Caribbean, but there were too many reminders of her loss. She wanted to go home. Today!

Brooke's cell phone vibrated in her pocket and then she heard a chirp. She recognized the familiar beeping ringtone she'd assigned to her parents. She answered. "Hello. You're early." Brooke noted it was seven a.m., which meant it was six o'clock in Charlotte.

"I wanted to get you before you left for work."

Resting an arm on the windowsill she said, "You made me nervous for a moment. I thought there might have been some kind of emergency."

"There is an emergency," Evelyn Jordan replied. "My daughter isn't going to be home for Christmas Eve dinner."

Brooke sighed. No one was more disappointed than she that on the only holiday her family emphatically made sure not to miss being together, she was four hours by plane away. There was just no way to get to Charlotte, actually have dinner with the family, and get back to the island on the same day. She had to work on Christmas Day.

"I'll be home for New Year's Eve," Brooke offered, knowing it was no consolation prize for the annual dinner with her grandmother, parents, six siblings, in-laws and nieces and nephews. She would be the only one missing this year. Her brother, Gage, had returned from a tour in Afghanistan and would be with the family for the first time in two years. Her heart ached and she knew it wasn't just about the family dinner. She'd been away from her family and friends for far too long. With the ridiculous hours she had to put in on the project, she hadn't had much time to even socialize and meet other people. Not that she probably would have taken the time to do that either. Brooke was on the verge of sliding into a state of depression and she knew it.

"Is the company sponsoring a dinner for the staff?"

Brooke moved through the large living room of the corporate apartment and entered the kitchen to start the coffeemaker.

"No. Everyone is gone. I mean the people who are still here live on the island. The ex-pats are home. There are two analysts and me. We don't need more. We babysit the system."

"Well, maybe you can make dinner. You could invite the analysts. Is one of them nice looking?"

Brooke shook her head. Not more match making. "Mother." Using mother was a sign that she was getting annoyed.

"I'm sorry. I was wondering if a change in environment might…" her mother stopped herself. "Never mind that. You could invite them anyway. People get lonely during the holidays."

Brooke didn't respond. People get lonely at Christmas. Forget people. She was lonely. Last year, she was married. Now, she was divorced. Last year, she was with her family. This year, she would be alone. Last year, she was pregnant. This year, she had no child. She didn't care about what other people needed. She had needs of her own.

"Sweetheart, don't they kind of work for you?" her mother's voice broke through her thoughts.

"Not technically. I'm the team leader. It's not the same as being the boss." Brooke fought to keep a sigh inside. She had explained the nature of her work to her mother several times, but for some reason the details weren't processing. "Anyway, we can't eat together. First off, one has a girlfriend he's spending time with and the other guy is, I don't know, anti-social. I hardly know him. Secondly, if I'm home, they're managing the system. We have to be there for the eighteen hours of the day that we're up."

"It seems such a waste not to be able to entertain. You have that big place and the kitchen is lovely."

Brooke did a visual sweep of the space. Her mother was right. She was in a two-bedroom apartment that actually slept six adults comfortably. The kitchen was fully equipped with every modern convenience a person could use. The community had three swimming pools, a hot tub, sauna, a fitness center and it had the added bonus of being directly on the beach with gulf views from nearly every window she'd seen. The company had spared no expense and Brooke was glad. The hotel she had lived in for the first few weeks had gotten old fast.

"I'm not interested in cooking for myself. Freeze a plate for me. I'll eat it when I get home. There are more than enough restaurants for me to stop in at. You know I love the local food."

Her mother conceded. "Okay, sweetie, I know you have to get to the office, so I'll let you go. What time will you be home this evening?"

"Same as always. Around eight."

"You've been working too hard."

"I make good money and I like my job. I can Skype with you guys during dinner. It'll be like I'm there."

Brooke heard the smile in her mother's voice. "It will. I'll take that. Your grandmother reminded me that I need not complain. I have living children. That's a blessing."

She smiled at her grandmother's wisdom and the not so subtle message behind it. "Stop complaining when you're blessed." That's what she always said when Brooke moaned about something.

The coffee maker beeped and she received a text

message from her driver that he was outside. "Gotta go. Love you, Mama and tell Daddy I love him too."

"Oh, Brooke, there's one more thing."

She knew it. Her mother never called this early in the morning unless something was up. "Sam called."

Brooke rolled her eyes.

"I didn't want to bring it up. It's not the first time." Her mother paused. "I thought you should know."

Brooke swallowed her contempt and tried to keep her voice even. "Thanks, Mama. I received an email. I'll go ahead and see what it says."

"That's probably a good idea," her mother said. "Have a good day, baby."

Brooke forced a smile into her voice. "I will."

They ended the call. She'd lied to her mother. Brooke had already deleted the email without opening it, and she'd deleted the others that came before that one. She pushed thoughts of Sam Riley from her mind the same way she pushed the delete button. She was not going to let rancid memories ruin her day.

She poured her coffee, popped the lid on her travel mug, grabbed her bags and left the apartment.

"Good mornin', Ms. Brooke." Desmond, the company's fulltime driver, opened the door to the company van and helped her into the back row.

"You're cheery this morning," Brooke replied getting settled into her seat.

He closed the door and went around to the front and climbed inside. "It's almost Christmas," Desmond shrieked happily. "Can you believe it'll be here in less than two days?"

Brooke took a long sip of her coffee and bit her lip after

she felt the sting of the burn. It was still too hot. "I've never been away from home for Christmas, so it doesn't really feel like it to me."

Desmond shrugged like her woes meant nothing. "Christmas is wherever you are. You get a tree and play some Christmas music and make a little holiday for yourself."

Brooke chuckled. "A tree?"

"They have plenty in the market. If you want, I can pick one out and set it up for you when you come home this evening. It's no trouble."

Brooke smiled. Desmond very respectful and professional, but he had been trying to get in her apartment for some reason or another ever since she arrived on the island.

"There's a nice tree in the lobby and another out on the beach. We have one at work that I can enjoy too. It's not a big deal." She pressed her coffee cup against her lips and her lie and looked out the window for the remainder of the drive from her apartment to the office building. The trip was less than three miles, but it took thirty minutes because Montego Bay's traffic was gridlocked. Just like it was at home in Charlotte. Where there was work, there was congestion. She surmised you couldn't escape it.

They turned off of Sunset Boulevard onto Southern Cross Boulevard. Desmond pulled in front of the tall, 55,000 square foot complex that was the home for Global Computer Systems. GCS provides business process outsourcing and information technology solutions for commercial and government clients. Brooke's position as business analyst was to maintain the servers that processed electronic benefit card transactions for a government nutrition program. The client's customers had access to the benefits on their cards 24 hours a day, so the system had to be online 24-7 or it was a customer service nightmare. They'd had those nightmares in the past. In order to ensure that the company didn't lose the government contract, GCS went through a massive technological upgrade in all the offices where they outsourced, which included this location.

Desmond opened the door on her side. Brooke stepped out and reached in for her bags.

"Would you like me to come get you for lunch?"

"No thanks, I'll get something up the street," she replied referring to the multitude of area restaurants she had to choose from.

"You text me if you change your mind about that tree."

She smiled. "Not likely, even if I were inclined, I don't have time."

"You do keep long hours, but at least you have some more help today."

Brooke wasn't sure what he meant by that. She tilted her head forward. "More help?"

"I picked a gentleman up at the airport last night."

Brooke wasn't aware of anyone else joining them. She wondered who had been given the daunting task of showing up the day before Christmas Eve. She knew she was being replaced in a few days so she could go home for a week, possibly for good. But she'd assumed the coworker that was replacing her wouldn't arrive until after Christmas. She also knew it was a woman, not a man.

She was way too curious to wait to find out who the mystery person was. She took a few steps toward Desmond and asked, "Do you remember his name?"

"I don't. I was told to meet him and hold up the company card," Desmond said. "It was late and he had to take a connection in from Kingston, so he was tired. He fell asleep in the car on the way from the airport."

Brooke nodded. If he'd flown to Kingston, he hadn't come from the Charlotte office.

Desmond continued. "He was here before, I think. But, he either walked to work or rented a car. I didn't drive him."

Brooke shrugged. "I guess I'll find out today."

"In a few minutes," Desmond added. "He asked for an even earlier call than you, so he's already here."

Brooke nodded again. "Thanks for the heads up. I'll see you later."

Desmond smiled. As was his habit, he climbed in and waited for her to clear the entrance of the building. As she was coming in, Brooke caught sight of a woman that she'd seen many times in the square near the restaurants and shopping areas. She appeared to be homeless on most days, choosing to sit on the ground or lie on the waist high concrete walls that enclosed the main walking areas. Two of the security guards had her, one under each arm and were escorting her out of the building.

One of them tipped his hat and the other greeted her, "Good morning, Ms. Jordan. I already turned the key in the elevator, so you can go right up."

"What's going on?" Brooke felt sorry for the woman. She looked like they were manhandling her a bit.

"She knows there's no trespassing," the other guard replied.

"Wait." Brooke stopped in front of them. She reached into her handbag and took out some Jamaican dollars she'd had converted from U.S. currency. It was more than enough to feed the woman for several days.

"Ma'am, no need," the guard stated.

"I know you're doing your job, but please turn her

loose," Brooke insisted. They did as they were instructed. Brooke took the woman's hand and pressed the money into it. "Get something to eat okay."

The woman looked down at the bills and cackled. "I thank you, Ms. Brooke, but I'm not hungry."

Brooke was taken back. Her first name. "How do you know---?"

"I heard the people you work with call you that," she said. "You've got a good heart. God is going to bless you with love."

Brooke opened her mouth to speak, but then closed it when she realized she didn't really have anything to say. Brooke was a bit uncomfortable with the lady's words, especially since she was a stranger that appeared to need someone to speak into her own disheveled life, but she wasn't going to assume that God wasn't using her. What was that scripture her grandmother quoted about "entertaining angels unaware"? So even though she'd simply wanted to make sure the woman ate and wasn't thrown out like trash by the security guards, Brooke paused to consider the stranger's words.

"Any idea where I'm going to find this love?" Brooke asked as she fought to hide the hint of sarcasm that threatened to coat her tone.

"You've already found it," the woman replied, "just give a little and life will give back."

Brooke had no idea what she could be talking about. Other than giving out of her wallet as she just had, there wasn't any other opportunity for her to share with anyone. Brooke nodded her understanding and watched the woman push through the revolving door and exit onto the street.

One of the guards escorted her to the waiting elevator and continued to hold the doors open while she stepped in.

"She's a crazy lady. Been cuckoo since I was a kid. Keep your money the next time."

Brooke supposed the guards were right. They would certainly know better than she. But her grandmother had taught her that if we have the time of day for a dog, we have it for each other. Besides, the money was nothing. She made plenty.

The elevator doors closed. She pushed the button for the fourth floor of the building where the offices for I.T. were housed. The main server was on the basement level. The three intervening floors comprised a call center. Those spaces were empty today, because it was Sunday. Very few call center staff worked on Sunday and those that did were in the United States offices.

Brooke heard her cell phone beep. She reached into her purse to remove it and felt a sharp bump against the bottom of the elevator car right before it paused. The elevator seemed to reboot and start again. She made a mental note to tell security to contact building maintenance and a second note to remind herself to use the other elevator until they fixed the problem. She looked down at her phone, opened the text message and read the words:

Aren't you usually at your desk by now?

Her heart started racing. She cleared the screen and dropped the phone back into her purse. The elevator doors opened. The late night arrival Desmond had spoken of…

"Good morning, Brooke. I've missed you."

Brooke let out a long breath. Christmas just got upgraded to ratchet.

About the Author

Rhonda McKnight is the author of the *Black Expressions* Top 20 bestseller, *A Woman's Revenge* (Mar 2013), *What Kind of Fool* (Feb 2012), *An Inconvenient Friend* (Aug 2010) and *Secrets and Lies* (Dec 2009). She was a 2010 nominee for the *African-American Literary Award* in the categories of Best Christian Fiction Novel and Best Anthology. She was the winner of the 2010 *Emma Award* for Favorite Debut Author and the 2009 *Shades of Romance Award* for Best Christian Fiction Novel. Originally from a small, coastal town in New Jersey, she's called Atlanta, Georgia home for fifteen years. Visit her at www.rhondamcknight.net and www.facebook.com/booksbyrhonda and join her Facebook reading group for discussions about her books at https://www.facebook.com/groups/rhondamcknight/

Books by Rhonda McKnight

What Kind of Fool

Feb 2012

The Wife, Her Husband. Their faith. . . . Will it save them before it's too late, or will an enemy from their past destroy their marriage forever?

Angelina Preston tunes out the voice of God when she decides to divorce her husband, Greg. She's forgiven him for his affair, but she won't forget, even though her heart is telling her to. Shortly after she files divorce papers, she finds out her non-profit organization is being investigated by the IRS for money laundering. In the midst of the very public scandal, Angelina becomes ill. Through financial and physical trials, she learns that faith and forgiveness may really be the cure for all that ails her, but can she forgive the people who hurt her most?

Sexy, successful Dr. Gregory Preston didn't appreciate his wife when he had her. His affair with a devious man-stealer has him put out of his home and put off with women who continue to throw themselves at him. Greg wants his wife back, but he'll have to do some fancy operating to get her. When the secrets and lies from his past continue to mess up his future, Greg finds himself looking to the God he abandoned long ago for a miracle only faith can provide.

Samaria Jacobs finally has the one thing she's always wanted: a man with money. The fact that she's in love with him is a bonus, but even so, life is anything but blissful. She's paying for her past sins in ways she never imagined and living in fear that the secret she's keeping will separate them forever.

An *Inconvenient* Friend

Aug 2010

Samaria Jacobs has her sights set on Gregory Preston. A successful surgeon, he has just the bankroll she needs to keep her in the lifestyle that her credit card debt has helped her grow accustomed to. Samaria joins New Mercies Christian Church to get close to Gregory's wife. If she gets to know Angelina Preston, she can become like her in more than just looks, and really work her way into Greg's heart.

Angelina Preston's life is filled with a successful career and busy ministry work, but something's just not right with her marriage. Late nights, early meetings, lipstick- and perfume-stained shirts have her suspicious that Greg is doing a little more operating than she'd like. But does she have the strength to confront the only man she's ever loved and risk losing him to the other woman? Just when Samaria thinks she's got it all figured out, she finds herself drawn to Angelina's kindness. Will she be able to carry out her plan after she finds herself yearning for the one thing she's never had . . . the friendship of a woman?

Made in the USA
San Bernardino, CA
15 September 2014

Secrets and Lies

Dec 2009

Faith Morgan is struggling with her faith. Years of neglect leave her doubting that God will ever fix her marriage. When a coworker accuses her husband, Jonah, of the unthinkable, Faith begins to wonder if she really knows him at all, and if it's truly in God's will for them to stay married.

Pediatric cardiologist Jonah Morgan is obsessed with one thing: his work. A childhood incident cemented his desire to heal children at any cost, even his family, but now he finds himself at a crossroads in his life. Will he continue to allow the past to haunt him, or find healing and peace in a God he shut out long ago?